W9-BYL-873

THE
RAKE

ALSO BY WILLIAM F. BUCKLEY JR.

THE
RAKE

A Novel

William F. Buckley Jr.

 HarperCollins*Publishers*

FIC
Buckley

This book is a work of fiction. References to real people, events, or locales are intended only to provide a sense of authenticity, and are used fictitiously. All other characters, and all incidents and dialogue, are drawn from the author's imagination and are not to be construed as real.

HarperCollins books may be purchased for educational, business, or sales promotional use. For information please write: Special Markets Department, HarperCollins Publishers, 10 East 53rd Street, New York, NY 10022.

FIRST EDITION

Designed by Laura Lindgren

Library of Congress Cataloging-in-Publication Data is available upon request.

ISBN: 978-0-06-123855-0

07 08 09 10 11   DIX/RRD 9 8 7 6 5 4 3 2 1

For Alexandra and Roger Kimball
With affection

THE
RAKE

BOOK ONE

PROLOGUE

Letellier, Manitoba, October 1991

Aucune possibilité de rien sauver!

No qualifications were set on the operation. Just this: there must be no chance that anything could survive the flames.

Anything? Like what?

Jean-Claude did not like to waste time asking himself questions he had no way of answering. Especially questions the answers to which were none of his business. His employer, Benoît, hadn't been talking about human beings. He had clearly been talking about some special object—whatever it was—that someone might want to save, might hope to rescue from the fire.

They would find nothing.

Oh, stop talking to yourself. If you have to talk, talk to Lucien.

But Lucien never has anything to say, at least not anything interesting. It pays just to repeat instructions: *This fire. It must destroy the entire building.* It is to be lit a half hour after the last lamp in the house is turned off. The inhabitants will then have the opportunity (possibilité) to get out. But not enough time to hunt for this or that object in the building to save it from the fire.

What is critical, then, is the timing. After that light goes off—Jean-Claude looked up to the rectory's second floor—Lucien will begin applying the creosote on the south side, while I do the east side.

Allow five minutes.

The next five minutes, he will be doing the west side; I, the north side, the garage side.

We reconvene exactly ten minutes after we began. Then we wait until thirty minutes have passed. If any light in the house should suddenly flash back on, the schedule is moved forward—to begin from when that light goes off again.

At hit time, Lucien does the south side, after that the west side; I'll be working east and north. We then go directly to the car and drive east five kilometers to the campsite. Pull in, set up the tent, arrange the fishing gear alongside. We're just sportsmen on a pleasant night out. My police radio, indispensable to fishermen for official notices, will bring in the police and fire reports. My guess is that even at that distance, we'll be able to spot the fire.

"Lucien. Lucien! I said to rest on your seat. I didn't tell you to go to sleep. From where we are parked we can make out the target clearly." He looked down at the dashboard. "It is just past 2200. We can expect that the lights will be turned off—"

"When?"

"How do I know when? It depends on who is living there, what their habits are." He let out a chuckle. "One hopes they do not sleep too heavily. Voilà! The light on the ground floor has been turned off. We have to hope that the light on the second floor isn't just the television. If it is, then—after waiting a while—we'll have to go to work even before that light is doused.

We'll have to assume whoever is watching television has gone to sleep. I'll make that decision if the light is still on at 2300. Understand?"

"J'ai faim."

"Then take one of the sandwiches. That's what they're for. That, and for breakfast."

Jean-Claude started to twirl the dial on the police radio, to assure himself that it was working.

Nothing worth listening to. Not yet. "Well, let's assume the second-floor light is still on at 2300, and we begin our operation then. At 2340 we light the inflammables. Back in the car by 2345. We pull in to the campsite by 2355. We'll pick something up on the radio at that point, I figure."

"Tu me parles?"

"No. I was talking to myself. And keeping my eye on the second-floor light."

CHAPTER 1

Grand Forks, North Dakota, September 1969

Last Saturday, after the ardent petting—after the movie, after the snack, after the giggles—Henrietta came to terms with what she knew, now, was Reuben's grand design. He was delicately concrete about it: it would take place in a duck blind. Not—he said with scorn—not at the Hop See Lodge. That was the handy motel across the river, in Minnesota. Hop See was a single-story caravansary in its second decade of operation. All that was required there of a patron was a driver's license and, of course, cash—fifteen dollars for twelve-hour access to a bedroom.

The Hop See also had conventional uses. Last November, during an overcrowded football weekend, Henri had booked a room there for Bruce Seringhaus, her young cousin. Bruce would share the room with another football fan, also in town for the game, from the University of Minnesota. The two would be strangers, but never mind. The other occupant would be duly registered with the University of North Dakota as a student from the visiting team's college looking for inexpensive lodging for the Saturday night, after the game.

Bruce was only eighteen, but he announced haughtily to his willowy twenty-year-old Canadian-born cousin that he was not willing to share "any old room" with "any old visitor" (never mind that he lived in shared quarters at his own university), "not even if he's a member of the football team. I'd rather sleep in the gym."

Henrietta soothed him by contributing half of the room's cost, allowing the stranger to be displaced. So Bruce had the Hop See room to himself, and he could have drowned his misery over the humiliation of his team's loss in solitude, except that he didn't drink.

Reuben scolded Henri for being extravagant, but she cut him off by saying she was certain he would have done the same thing if *he* had an eighteen-year-old cousin coming to town to see the big game without a place to stay. Reuben smiled indulgently and leaned over, in the common room, to give her a light kiss, spilling his curly blond hair over her blue eyes and slender nose.

So much for the Hop See. The idea of the duck blind in place of the motel appealed to her, though she felt a shaft of fear, and the dull pain of sin coveted, and acquiesced in.

Still, leave it to Reuben, dominant in all matters. He too was a senior, handsome, spare, and agile, at twenty-one a formidable figure in the student body. He lifted his head and smiled first with his eyes. Then his teeth flashed out. The grin was quick, mischievous. For Henrietta Leborcier it was captivating, a prologue to the momentous event, planned now for the following Saturday.

Reuben always had interesting ideas, she reminded herself as she sat across from him in the library. This one, Reuben confessed, had taken much of the summer to gestate. It was climactic, whatever else you might call the prospective surrender of your virginity. She looked up at him, his head bent over the book, his teeth gripping the eraser end of the pencil that dangled from his lips. A trace of a furrow could be seen on his forehead as he engaged the text. She crooked her finger, interlocked with his, and he looked over at her. He gave a wide-eyed smile, moving his book out of the way, as if removing anything that might stand between him and his Henrietta of the light brown hair, which framed her carelessly freckled oval face and blue eyes. He leaned over and, observing the solemn silence of the Chester Fritz Library, spoke in a whisper. They were seated in a corner of the large room, safely removed from the librarian's desk. Their requisitioned books were open on the table between them, and they each had one hand under the table, their handclasp shielded from casual view.

"Tell me more about the duck blind."

"Well sure, Henri!"

Reuben seemed not quite old enough to be a college student, let alone a senior. But his smile now managed a trace of cosmopolitan knowingness. He did not try to disguise his excitement over the plotted enterprise, just four days away, at Rico's father's duck blind.

Speaking in a husky whisper, he described the site. "The twin blinds are closed down except during duck season, and that runs from the end of September to sometime in November, maybe December. Rico—Eric—has been going out there with his dad ever since he was little, way before he could fire a gun, though he's pretty good at it now, he says. Says he got twelve ducks last season in two mornings of shooting. His dad owns

9

one blind, his dad's law partner, Al Knudson, the adjoining blind. They go out together pretty often during the season. The blinds are shut down the day the duck season ends—Monsanto & Knudson aren't about to break the law, though they're good at letting their clients get away with it."

"Don't be cynical, Reuben."

"What else do you think lawyers are for? Maybe I'll become a lawyer. If I do, you can go ahead and break any law you want. Anyway, Rico's dad and Al Knudson go hunting often—they're there for sure at dawn on the first day of the season. Ahead of that first outing, they send Rico—he started doing this in high school—to clean up the blinds and do a little provisioning."

Henri nodded pensively, though her thoughts were not on hunting.

Yes, she said after a pause, apart from everything else planned for that night, she was curious to lay eyes on a duck blind. "I've never been in one before. As a matter of fact, I don't...shoot ducks. Not yet. Maybe," she smiled, and flexed her finger, "I'll take up duck hunting after Saturday. Saturday. It'll be just us?"

"You and me, and Rico and his new girlfriend. No reason to keep them away—is there, Henri? You know we're talking about two *separate*—separated—blinds. They're adjoining, but there's a partition between them. So Eric will bring Linda—I don't think you've met her; nice young thing."

Henrietta winced. She wondered whether she too was a nice young thing.

"Rico's not going to let on to her, not until they're in the car, that he's planning to spend all night at the blind. She'll think it's just a visit. Linda will be surprised," he chuckled. "Though she wasn't looking, I'd guess"—he was speaking as if to himself—"to spend the night alone back in the dorm. But they'll be in the Monsanto blind. We'll be next door, in Knudson's blind."

"Will we actually see any ducks?"

"I dunno. Forget the ducks. You can always see ducks in the zoo."

"No, you can't, Reuben." *Darling dumb Reuben.* Sometimes he made her impatient. "Just because ducks don't vote doesn't mean you have to be that ignorant about them. There aren't any *ducks* in the zoo, stupid. No one would guess you were a . . . an experienced reporter, let alone editor in chief of the *Dakota Student*. Never mind. What are they like, the blinds?"

"I've never actually seen them. Rico says they're small but complete units. Each has a bed—or at least a mattress—behind the opening you stand up to shoot through. There's a partition between the two—I mentioned that. The hunters go out to the blinds the night before with their dog, a retriever, which has its own kennel outside. They set the alarm for an hour before dawn.

"The two blinds are laid out parallel. That gives the two hunters max view over the lake when the birds circle down. At the base, where the two blinds join, there's a table of some sort, where the hunters can eat. There are gaslights for illumination and a gas stove, Rico says, and basic kitchen stuff, and plenty of blankets, plus the bedrolls we'll bring. Outside they have a heavy canvas tent staked down, enclosing the pair of blinds. It's the color of dry reeds—camouflage. And it's zipped shut until time comes to look out for the birds. It doesn't get exactly hot in there during hunting season, Rico says, but the wind is blocked and the stove gives out a good amount of heat."

"Makes me shiver, just thinking about it."

Reuben stroked her hand. "Saturday night's not a time you'll be shivering. At least not from the cold." Reuben tightened his hold on her hand. For appearance's sake, he ostentatiously turned a page of the heavy book that lay before him. He would concentrate on the 1787 Philadelphia Convention some other time.

He spoke with the excitement of a boy—which he technically was, until "the day before yesterday," as Henri had referred to Reuben's twenty-first birthday in the letter to her father in Paris.

"There's a big old wooden icebox by the stove, Rico says. That would be empty now, in the off-season, but Rico's going to bring a couple of ice blocks and a few bottles of this and that to drink. We'll probably bring hot dogs we can fry, and rolls we can heat, and maybe a pumpkin pie or something. In the season the blinds would be stocked with Monsanto's and Knudson's booze, but Rico says if we want any we'll have to bring it." Reuben slipped a foot out of his moccasin, edging his toes onto her ankle. He offhandedly turned another leaf in his book.

Henri said, "When will we go to the blind? Only after the football game is over, right?"

"Of course, we can't miss the game. And I have to put in an appearance at the paper. The *Dakota Student* can't have its first party of the year without its editor in chief! Still, we should be able to get to the blind maybe eight, nine o'clock."

Again she nodded, in disciplined acquiescence. "And this is only Tuesday. Saturday's a long way off." She stopped herself. "I mean, actually it's just around the corner."

He turned his eyes from his book to her eyes. Her cheeks had reddened. "Scared?"

"Yes. Sort of.... Are *you* scared, Reuben?"

"Yes, I guess I am." But quickly his face lit up. "Maybe Rico and Linda will sort of beef us up!"

"Is he... an old hand?"

"Of course! Rico's twenty-three!"

She loosened her fingers from his and closed her book. She got up and walked with it to the librarian's great mahogany desk, with the green felt surface and the iron-gray containers for three-by-five cards.

Reuben's eyes followed her. But he didn't pursue her. Henrietta liked it about Reuben Castle that he knew when not to talk, when not to react defensively to her occasional withdrawals from the scene or to changes in her mood, usually tranquil. Sometimes, after one of her silences, she would search out what it was that had disturbed or distracted her, and perhaps try to talk it out with Reuben. Sometimes she would just let matters rest. This time she smiled to herself. She'd let matters rest and maybe talk to him later about what had to be done to end the war in Vietnam. Or to end ROTC on campus. Reuben Castle was the number one political protester at UND.

What would she think to say—to talk about—on Saturday night? They hadn't spoken together at all about how things would be, well, afterward. But she did wonder about it, wonder anxiously. What would it be like waking up on Sunday morning with a naked man in bed with her?

Reuben had himself thought about it in lascivious detail, but not without apprehension. He took refuge in a studied air of insouciance. Condescension could be useful. He grinned. Would Henrietta expect to be driven to Mass on Sunday?

He interrupted his irony with practiced ease. He loved that too about her, the sophisticated child of a widowed French professor, able to handle two worlds at once. Henri had lived half her young life in France, picking up from the French many of their habits, but not their inattention to the commandment to keep holy the Sabbath. Henrietta always went to church on Sundays, so there would be no surprises on that score for Reuben Castle, who thought nothing of it that she would be going from the duck blind to her church.

CHAPTER 2

Grand Forks, February 1967

In freshman year Reuben Castle had signed up to compete for a position on the *Dakota Student*. He resolved in a matter of days that, after duty served as a subordinate, he would one day contend for editor in chief. He was by nature competitive but also adroit about the expenditure of energy. Very early he reasoned that by a shrewd application of practical and psychological intelligence he could increase the prospects of success, while diminishing the pains of achieving it.

Elections for the senior positions on the *Dakota Student* were held in the spring, with juniors contending for the following year's top slots. Every junior on the staff had a vote. Reuben set himself the challenge of demonstrating his preeminence by the time junior year came around, demonstrating it not just by the discharge of his duties as associate editor but also by achievements in other campus activities. By May 1969 he'd be quite ready, he calculated while still a freshman, to take on the responsibilities of editor of the *Student*.

That position brought much prestige on campus. The paper, founded in 1888 as a monthly, became a weekly in 1904, and in 1928 it went to two issues every week. Its editor had been dubbed by the college president the "uncrowned king of the campus."

Reuben planned to receive such presidential deference one day. But now—spring term, 1967—he had to win one of the freshman slots. Aspirant journalists were expected to file two stories a week during the eight-week competition. They were also expected to forage for newspaper ads in the commercial corners of Grand Forks. There were 34,000 residents in Grand Forks, and 5,000 students at the University of North Dakota. "Never mind that ours is a small city, and that we have a small student body," the business manager of the *Dakota Student* said. He was lecturing the eighteen freshmen crowded into the *Student*'s pressroom for the briefing at the start of their competitive ordeal. "It won't get you into the *Student* if you write every day like Hemingway and do nothing else. We have to earn our keep—we have to pay for our paper, pay the printer. If you don't contribute to the business end, you're not going to make it."

Reuben raised his hand to ask a question. "Is there enough revenue here in Grand Forks for the ads we need"—a less assured freshman would have spoken of the ads "you" need—"or will we need to bring in ads from national advertisers?"

"We get some of those—you've obviously noticed the travel ads and the cigarette ads. But mostly—like eighty-five percent— it's local business we live on. Five thousand students means a lot of hamburgers eaten and a lot of blue jeans and movie tickets bought. Your job is to bring in advertisements from these businesses. If they're already advertising, get them to increase their commitments."

Reuben whispered to the intense young woman seated next

to him on the long bench: "Maybe we should get the student body to eat more hamburgers?" She did not acknowledge his crack—Maria Cervantes was fully occupied taking notes, listening first to the business manager, then to the editor.

The managing editor led the students around the newspaper's offices, then back to the well of the pressroom. The entire operation was lodged in one wing of the student union. The following Monday, the competitors would receive their first assignments at one-thirty and come back later in the afternoon with their research material. Using the paper's battered inventory of old manual typewriters, they would bang out their copy. They would spend two long nights at the paper every week, Monday and Thursday. Some would tear up draft after draft, the slower students desperate, in the early weeks especially, to prove that they could produce a publishable 400-word story on the prospects of the Fighting Sioux basketball team, or on the message of a visiting speaker, or on a student committee preparing for the national political campaign coming up in 1968.

Checking in on the first day, Reuben surveyed the scene in the pressroom, the same room in which he and the others had assembled the previous Friday. This time he ran his eyes about the room, paying utilitarian attention to details. He quietly decided, looking over a dozen typewriters, to appropriate as his own the Royal standard sitting in a corner under a dust cover. Immediately after the editor had given out assignments, Reuben rose (the competitors had sat cross-legged on the floor) and walked over to the Royal. He turned it upside down and reached into his pocket. Opening his penknife he gave the impression that he was tending to the Royal's innards.

It had the desired effect. The typewriter was taken to be the personal property of Reuben Castle. After wiping off the knife on a Kleenex, he sat down in front of the machine and started to type, his lips sealed, his eyes fastened on the stand that supported his notebook, his fingers moving confidently about the keyboard. ("Unless you can touch-type," at age fourteen he had informed his father, a carpenter, "you may as well forget about professional life.")

A freshman with thick glasses was looking about anxiously for an available typewriter. He had the air of a man with a scoop. But catching sight of Reuben, he paused to say, "You know your way around that typewriter, all right."

Reuben arrested his finger action and smiled. "I put a little oil in the machine yesterday and wanted to see how it was working out."

But yesterday had been Sunday. The *Dakota Student* office had been closed, the freshman competition not yet begun. What had Reuben Castle been doing in the paper's closed offices?

No one asked. There was something about Reuben that made the young people he mingled with uncomplainingly acquiescent in the things he did. This extended to stories he wrote, remarks he made, compliments he bestowed. Some of what he did, if done by others, might have been thought presumptuous or patronizing. Reuben managed to assume seniority without giving others any reciprocal sense of inferiority.

In a few weeks he was accepted as a junior master of the craft he was learning, so much so that some openly sought his counsel, submitting their own work for his comment. He helped them without suggesting that there was now a debt someday to be repaid. He accepted gratitude, spoken or intimated, as a nice expression of the bounties of life and of the amenities of the University of North Dakota.

One of the few people apparently immune to his easy charm was Maria Cervantes. She was a determined young woman from Fresno, at UND to study agricultural economics. Maria was immensely fortified by her calm resignation to the shapelessness of her body and the plainness of her face. She was resolutely indifferent to her appearance, but not to her work. During the freshman competition, when students were expected to file two stories each week, Maria regularly filed four. She also did more than her share on the advertising front. When the eight-week trial was over, Reuben Castle, Maria Cervantes, and Eric Monsanto were recognized as the brightest stars among the elated newly chosen staffers of the *Dakota Student*.

CHAPTER 3

Grand Forks, May 1969

As election day for senior positions on the *Student* approached, all eyes were on Reuben Castle. The national attention Zap Day had received and the ingenuity of his idea weren't lost on those who would be casting a ballot for editor in chief. They were— they prided themselves—journalists, after all.

It had been a smashing publicity coup, no doubt about it. But— was a stunt of that kind really appropriate for an aspirant editor in chief of the *Dakota Student*?

There were two schools of thought. The doubt worked to the advantage of Maria Cervantes. She was, in any case, the meritocratic favorite. Among the *Student*'s staff, Reuben had evolved from companion to demigod to colleague with alien interests. His critics looked on him primarily as the president, secretary, and treasurer of Reuben Castle, Inc. His labors for the *Student*, after his super-successful run in the freshman competition, had been irregular—flashy, episodic, and theatrical, culminating in Zap Day.

Maria, meanwhile, was a week-after-week performer, punctual, thorough, accomplished. She had the problem that she wasn't liked very much. Her comprehensive efficiency was accompanied by a certain sourness of disposition, though perhaps it was her prickliness that engendered her perfectionism. Shrewd judges on the senior staff doubted she would be elected. Eliminating her left as principal contenders Reuben, and Eric Monsanto—history major, partygoer, and UND enthusiast, who was fully conversant with the paper's commercial life.

Over a couple of beers at the Hop See Lodge's oily little bar, the outgoing editor spent an argumentative two hours with the outgoing business manager. Neither was (quite yet) twenty-one; still, they drank their beer safely at the Hop See. Minnesota had its blue laws, but like everything else undertaken at the Hop See, these laws were lightly observed. The dutiful monthly inspection by the Vice Lady (that was the name the student drinking community gave to Sergeant Lucille Grimmelfarb) took place without fail. She drove in to check up on the Hop See on the first Monday of the month, regularly, at six P.M., and in anticipation the bar was squeaky clean in its clientele. Elderly tipplers knew they could get a free drink from management on those Mondays, when their patronage was especially valued. Today was not a Vice-Lady Monday, so Jack Bergland quaffed his beer without fear of interruption. He reaffirmed to his partner in power and fellow lame duck, Eileen Sanborn, his conviction that Reuben Castle was the best prospect for editor of the *Student*.

"You can have him," Eileen said. "What I don't want is for you editorial people to reach over and draft our boy, Monsanto, to be editor. He's made to order for business manager. It did occur to you—didn't it, Jack?—that the *Dakota Student* depends rather heavily on advertising revenue for our publishing operation?"

"Yes. —Yes, dear." Jack retaliated against her condescending tone by calling attention to her sex. "And it may have occurred to *you*, Eileen, that advertisers want a student paper that's read, not a yellow page for the pizza houses."

"Okay okay. What do you want to quarrel about? It's fine by me if Reuben gets your chair. But once he becomes editor, I think you'll find he won't be spending a whole lot of time on the paper. He's in a hurry for something else."

"What else? They're not going to elect him mayor of Zap."

That brought a smile. "No. But, well—almost anything else. There are other mountains for Reuben to climb. He's too young to run for Congress. Maybe he'll crank up a constitutional amendment to remove the age limitation."

"So? On the matter of personal ambition, your boy Monsanto isn't going to spend all his life on the *Student* selling ads."

"I'm not saying he will. And I don't deny he'd rather be the editor than the business manager. But after the first ballot—which will probably put Castle in the lead—the office of business manager will beckon, and he'd be a fine manager." She looked up at Bergland. "But it's true, Jack. Rico *would* like to be editor."

"So would three other guys."

"And—if you don't mind—two girls."

When Castle's column appeared on that Tuesday in early March, it did indeed catch the attention of his fellow editors on the *Da-*

kota Student. But it caught, also, the attention of the entire student body, the entire town of Grand Forks, and by the end of the week what seemed like the entire world. *Zip to Zap!*

Spring of 1969 was a restless season. A million male students, coast to coast, were coming upon a drastic fork in the road. One choice entailed the risk of being drafted and perhaps sent to Vietnam. The other—a self-protective alternative—beckoned to prolonged academic life, beyond what most of the young men in question had anticipated as freshmen, or desired as seniors, but keeping them out of reach of the draft boards.

The disposition of the majority of activist students, male and female, was to seek out sites at which to publicize their protests. At Harvard, a six-day strike initiated by Students for a Democratic Society called for the admission of more minority students, the expansion of minority studies, and the abolition of university-sponsored ROTC. Official Harvard soon capitulated. Harvard's administration pledged also to keep the door open to student protesters.

To the activists, these were steps in the right direction. But on the national scene, appetites were not slaked. EXTRACURRICULAR GENOCIDE IS STILL GENOCIDE, one popular placard read. At CCNY, in New York, students blocked access to the campus. But few protests were as ingenious as the one in Grand Forks back in January, when the Students for Non-Violent Action called on everyone to tune in to the hated Richard Nixon's inauguration as president of the United States. When he reached the words "So help me God," everyone was to flush the nearest toilet. "We hope," the SNVA's circular announced, "to flush the toilets not only of all the dorms, apartments, and lecture halls in and around the campus, but also of downtown hotels, restaurants, high schools, and private homes." An alarmed city engineer called a press conference to warn that, there being more than 10,000 toilets in Grand Forks, "if they are all flushed at the same time, the pressure would break the pipelines."

Reuben was of course a leading protester. When he sat down at his Royal standard one day in March to write his weekly column, he thought to fuse two engines of student concern: national affairs and social life. "I've been thinking"—Reuben's column began—"and when I think, well, it makes me want to do things. And what I thought about yesterday was the scene at Fort Lauderdale. (That's Fort Lauderdale, Florida, you jerks.)

"The scene there is big stretches of sand, warm sea water, and beer. You spend your days on the beach and have beers at lunch, and maybe before lunch, and certainly before dinner, and after dinner. This week's issue of *Life* magazine says there'll be maybe a quarter million students going down to Florida for the sun and for a relaxing time with other young Americans who know how to look after themselves. And have the means to do it."

Reuben then surveyed the travel options.

"For the affluent, you can travel by airplane—Grand Forks to Minneapolis, then to Chicago, then Miami—and then catch a bus from Miami to Fort Lauderdale. Cost: $227. That'll buy you about half a semester of classes at UND.

"Sure, you can do it for less if you travel by rail, same route.

"Or you can do it by bus, same route, forty-one hours.

"Or, if you've got connections, you can borrow your favorite parents' less-than-favorite car, sign on three buddies, split the costs, and drive away." Reuben designated to the printer, on the typewritten copy, that at the end of that paragraph, a typographical "dingbat," as compositors call little decorative ornaments, should appear in bold face. In the ensuing paragraph he plunged excitedly into his proposal:

"I say: Nuts to people who feel that to have any fun or to voice protests they need to go to Florida. Where we should go is—*Zap*!

"You're asking yourselves, Where is Zap? Well, Zap is in the center of our glorious state. It has a population not of 83,000, like Fort Lauderdale. Not of 34,000, like Grand Forks. But of 450! It's in a valley and there's a creek that runs though the middle of town. Zap is just twelve miles south of Lake Saka-kawea. Boys and girls, here we come!"

He paused to deliberate such ancillary questions as would probably suggest themselves to his readers.

"What will we do after we have zipped to Zap? We'll celebrate a lot of things—including our independence from the Fort Lauderdale crowd. We'll protest the Vietnam War. We'll protest the anti-missile missiles—the ABMs—they're planning to put down in our state. We'll call for removing ROTC from the campus."

There were practical questions, granted: "Where will we eat? Sleep?

"Well, we'll ask the farmers there with their great spreads to let us camp out. We'll need lots of things for the big weekend besides shelter. We'll need music. Lots of music. Lots of beer. Lots of hamburgers, maybe French fries, if anybody can figure out how to make these in the wild North Dakota spring. Maybe a Red Cross station for you jerks who get carried away. Yes, we'll need a lot of things."

Another typographical embellishment preceded his final paragraph.

"Which is why," he concluded, "I'm going to launch the Zip to Zap committee. Objective: A great three-day party in Zap, starting on May 2, when spring is really here. I need volunteers now to help organize everything. Write me at UND Box 1137, or call me at 777-2166. I'll meet with the early-bird volunteers—Zippers to Zap!—this Saturday, nine A.M., to get things started."

Friday's was a great party. Over 3,000 students went to Zap. They ate their hamburgers, and drank their beer, and listened to three bands of musicians who performed using huge loudspeakers. The hospitality of the farmers was accepted, and soon abused. On Saturday it turned cold, much colder than was normal for early May. There wasn't enough food, though the beer supply was somehow uninterrupted. The good-hearted little Zap Café distributed Zapburgers but quickly ran out. Wood was torn from derelict barns to build fires to mitigate the cold. The national networks sent crews.

Saturday evening, at an emergency meeting, Zap's councilmen retreated from their official welcome and urged the students to go home. But the students weren't ready to go home. They sat, in their parkas and overcoats, and listened to the bands, huddling close together to stay warm.

At daybreak on Sunday, 500 members of the National Guard drove into Zap, responding to the first "riot" ever officially recorded in North Dakota. The crowds ebbed away. The town of Zap had suffered damage amounting to $25,000. On Tuesday,

Castle's column led off with a public apology for the misconduct. He volunteered a personal contribution of $100 to make amends for what the Zippers had overdone. "Where did you find $100?" Rico asked him. He knew that Reuben's father, the self-employed carpenter, paid his son's school bills and provided a monthly allowance of only $50. "You been rolling dice again?"

"No, Rico. I just took it from the paper's cash box."

Eric Monsanto smiled and backed off. Not his business. Besides, Reuben Castle, on the eve of the *Dakota Student* election, was very nearly a national figure, the greatest entrepreneur in recent UND history. But he was also a statesman, willing to accept a share of blame, stepping forward to effect restitution.

The following Monday, the *Dakota Student* staff elected Reuben Castle editor in chief, and Eric Monsanto business manager.

CHAPTER 4

Grand Forks, May 1969

Eileen Sanborn was right about the mountains Reuben Castle was bent on climbing. Two days after he was elected editor of the *Dakota Student* he announced that he was a candidate for chairman of the Student Council.

Student reaction to that announcement came in stages. Most students weren't particularly interested in extracurricular activities, except for following the UND sports teams. But some were, and among them the first reaction was one of slight weariness. (*Oh, God, Castle rides again.*) That developed, among some politically active students, into a fatalistic resentment. There was nothing to be done about it: Reuben Castle was... special. Though apparently carefree, he was earnest in his ambition to lead his class. He was also an effective controversialist, an accomplished journalist.

About a week before the Student Council election, Harold Blest withdrew his name as a candidate, followed three days later by Barbara Severson, who said she would be marrying and leaving school. That left Reuben all but alone to compete for the office. Most of his classmates simply accepted that Castle was a young man destined to make his way in life. The chairmanship of the UND Student Council was just the next rung in the long climb ahead. "The manifest destiny of the student body," a junior editor teased in an otherwise solemn endorsement of Castle, "is not to question the path of the comet that crosses our sky. We should just look at it, and say we're glad we had a glimpse of it." By the time Reuben was elected chairman, his status as big man on campus was taken for granted. After his success in getting the university to ban ROTC, he was energetically applauded in ideological circles.

Among other things, Reuben's election gave him the use of the university station wagon every other Sunday, provided it hadn't been reserved for official purposes. Sometimes it was needed to cart stage settings to or from the Burtness Theater; it was used every now and then to meet, or dispatch, university guests at the Grand Forks airport or to take especially august figures (this service was most often used by visiting trustees) as far away as to the airport in Minneapolis. But barring such preemptions, Sunday possession of the car alternated between Reuben and Sally Paulsen, the outgoing Student Council chairman. Once he was formally inaugurated next fall Reuben would inherit use of the car every Sunday until May, when his successor was elected and the car sharing began afresh.

A group of students belonging to the activist Students for a Democratic Society planned a little commotion for the big day in October when the new Student Council and its officers would be sworn in. SDS had in mind something that would draw attention to protests against the war and against the deployment of anti-missile missiles in North Dakota. The college station wagon would play an auxiliary role in the proceedings.

Reuben's inaugural committee had made up a large red ribbon, a foot wide and sixty feet long, bearing gold lettering: "GOOD LUCK CLASS OF 1970!" The three girls in charge of decorations would drape the ribbon around the station wagon while it was still offstage. The antiwar activists planned to swoop down on the vehicle with their own banner, overshadowing the official one. It would read, "STUDENTS AT PEACE—FOR PEACE."

The festivities always began almost immediately after the hockey game ended, shortly before six P.M. In days gone by, the station wagon would drive onto the rink loaded with kegs of beer. The beer would be unloaded and joyfully consumed while the band played, ending with the college anthem, "Stand Up and Cheer," students standing and singing out the chorus. Testimonials would be exchanged, and the station wagon would slide around the rink, pushed here and there by students on ice skates. The players on the visiting hockey team happily participated, and the band reciprocated by playing the anthem of the visitors' college.

The proceedings always featured a mystery guest, sitting in the passenger seat of the station wagon, face hidden by a great green-and-white shawl. Everyone waited eagerly for the opening of the station-wagon door. Only the incoming chairman knew who would be stepping out. Last year it was the good-natured president of UND, George Starcher, wearing a fake mustache. Once it had been Miss America, once a caged lion, and the year before that the movie actress Estelle Linkletter. The cheerleaders would greet the mystery guest with enthusiasm and excitement. When Reuben was an awestruck freshman he would not have been surprised if John Lennon had emerged as the mystery guest.

But suddenly, in October 1968, there was no more beer. The easygoing neglect of the state's blue law against supplying beer to minors had caught the attention of a law-and-order trustee—unhappily, a year-round resident of Grand Forks. Kurt Reuger was a devotee of UND affairs. He was capable of showing up at just about any scheduled student function. When he appeared, students would rue the day they were born, if that had been less than twenty-one years earlier and if they were detected with a glass of beer by Mr. Reuger's vigilance.

The enforcement of the beer prohibition generated widespread resentment. "May as well blame it on LBJ," Reuben had said to Henri, over a beer at the Hop See. "It's the American way—blame everything on the chief bad guy."

"Yes," Henri nodded, her face solemn, but her eyes sparkling. "Blame him for the Vietnam War, the ABM program, and the rise in the cost of living."

"That's what we call ideological opportunism," Reuben said, sipping his beer with delight. Reuben allowed himself to be carried away on the theme of LBJ. "You know, just imagine—*just suppose*—that Sally had thought to convey an invitation to the White House and that LBJ had *accepted*! The mystery guest comes out of the station wagon and it's *the president of the United States*! Henri, I'm not sure he'd have gotten out of there alive."

"That's silly, Reuben. Dumb. The president can come and go without your permission."

"Of course—though I've done my bit to restrict his movements. You know that."

Indeed she did. Against her advice Reuben had marched in Chicago with the thousands of other protesters at the Democratic convention in August 1968. President Johnson, having decided not to run for reelection, had appropriately declined to attend. But Reuben was one of the agitators who had gone one step too far, ending up in jail after the police cracked down at Lincoln Park. He had asked the resolute cop who led him into the police station whether the jail had any postcards—"I'd like to send some to my friends." Reuben winced at the memory. "That's when he clubbed me."

"I don't blame him," Henri said.

Inauguration Day 1969 was a festive day on campus. Henrietta wore her fake-fur coat and held up a UND banner, green and white, mounted on a three-foot-long stick. She was seated in the crowded stands two or three rows up from the improvised ceremonial stage. Reuben had wanted her to sit in the box with the student dignitaries, but she said no. "Reuben, I haven't belonged to anything much here, and I've certainly never been president or chairman of anything—"

"I was going to suggest you appear as honorary chairman of the Duck Hunters' League."

Henri blushed lightly and turned her head, but Reuben had already darted away to see to his myriad duties.

She watched it all from her seat in the stands, looking down at the student powerhouses engaged in yielding authority, and assuming authority—early training in democratic discipline? After the preliminaries, Reuben was sworn in. He gave a five-minute speech on the moral responsibility of college students to be active in the development of national policy. Henri cheered and applauded as Reuben promised the end of the Vietnam War, a repeal of the Sentinel missile emplacements, expedited student loans, and the elevation of water hockey to NCAA status. "As for my predecessor"—he had turned to Sally Paulsen, seated alongside—"let's cheer that she's a girl—and won't ever have to fly off to fight an illegal war in Vietnam."

All eyes turned to the outgoing chairman with the wrestler's build, an ardent supporter of Lyndon Johnson and the Vietnam War. Henri found herself relieved when, after an instant's dramatic deliberation, Sally laughed. Henri laughed in turn: it would have been a memorable scene if, taking offense, Sally had sprung from her seat and lunged at Reuben. Sally was captain of the UND women's volleyball team.

Then the moment came for the station wagon and the red ribbons, and the mystery guest. He turned out to be the aged campus hero Bronson Reid, Class of 1911. Reid had been an Olympic athlete the year after graduating, but now he had trouble stepping out of the car.

It was a heady couple of hours. By eight o'clock, half of the skating rink had been covered with squares of plywood, turning it into a dance floor. The big brassy UND band gave way to a rock band, and the undergraduates filled the rink with their gyrations. It didn't hurt that beer was somehow getting around. Sally Paulsen, freed of formal responsibilities as chairman of the Student Council, offered toast after solemn toast in honor of Kurt Reuger.

CHAPTER 5

Grand Forks/Letellier, November 1969

After the football game, Reuben led Henri to the gateway and out to the station wagon, which he laid claim to, even though it wasn't quite yet Sunday. He suggested they pop over to the Hop See for a nightcap, but Henri kissed him and said she was going home. "I'm tired. We'll have a good day tomorrow. A special day. I promise." She kissed him again, and walked away toward her dorm.

She went to Mass at Saint Michael's Church at nine. When she came out, Reuben was there with the sparkling station wagon he had himself washed and waxed. He was standing by the passenger door, leaning back against the car, dressed in a blue sweater and chinos, as usual jaunty and cocked for action, whether pleasurable or professional, and often he didn't see a difference between the two.

He didn't know it, but it would be a grave day for him—and for her. She had planned all the details as carefully as a general would plan an amphibious landing. But she had not acted alone. She had prayed for guidance and was resolved now on the correctness of her plans.

So where would they go in their official car, this sunny November day? Henrietta spoke quietly but with unmistakable resolution. "I told you, honey. Three days ago. I want to go to Letellier. It's ten miles across the border in Manitoba. I explained that to you."

"Oh, yes. That's where your mom was from."

"Yes. And where I was born."

They drove off, and Reuben settled the car down at sixty miles per hour as they headed up the Red River Valley. Reuben liked to play the date game, which was making the rounds on campus among the livelier students. "So that was 1948, the year you were born. What else happened in 1948 that was newsworthy?"

"Well, let's see." Henri rolled the window up, to hear better. "That was the year the Communists made a big bid for power in Italy."

"And in France."

"Well, yes. And in France. Was I supposed to say 'in Italy and in France'? Like I had forgotten about France?" She was mildly annoyed, but glad to be diverted from the important business at hand. "I wasn't set to come up, Reuben, with what happened *everywhere* in 1948. That might have been a big year in Mongolia, for all I know. Are you going to go on with this?"

"Yeah," he said, pulling out to pass the big truck. "What about 1848?"

"That was the short unhappy reign of Louis XVIII, wasn't it?"

"I'll give you that. Europe is your thing. Mine's America."

"Okay, what happened in the good old USA in 1848? By the way, did you ever take a course with Professor Benning?"

"No. Why?"

Henri's face turned grave, her voice that of a fussy class-room lecturer. "He said he overheard two women talking in an airplane. One of them asked, 'Why did we have to pay for Louisiana when we got the other states free?' "

"What was the reason?" Reuben sounded genuinely per-plexed.

"The other woman explained. She said those territories were owned by two sisters, Louise and Anna Wilmot. They agreed to give the land to the Union provided it was named after them. That was the Wilmot Proviso. But Winfield Scott refused to go along. That was the Dred Scott decision."

Henri laughed happily, as did Reuben. But she didn't go on with the running badinage. She fell silent as they made their way through the rich farmlands. The fields were now brown, and there were patches of snow. Reuben had gotten used to her occasionally opting for silence. Finally he spoke. "That exit was our last chance to avoid Canada," he teased. Reuben liked it when conversation ensued after a prod from him, as usually it did. But all he got from Henri now was a perfunctory acknowl-edgment—yes, Canada lay directly ahead. That was all she said.

What Henrietta now wanted was just to get on with the trip. The oblique autumn sun made the hills with their leafless trees just a little forbidding. Reuben was quiet for five minutes. Then he turned on the radio. The news report told of two U.S. infantry regiments dispatched for reinforcement duty in Vietnam.

Breaking the silence Henri said, "You take the next exit, in two miles, and then turn left."

"Left it is. What would happen if I turned right? Bump into a Nixon rally?"

She smiled, but said nothing.

The border crossing was routine.

"Where are you headed? Winnipeg?" The Canadian officer leaned down, addressing Reuben.

"Actually, we're going to Letellier. My girl—my lady friend was born in Letellier."

The guard peered over to view Henri. "Well, I'm sure, miss, they were sorry to see you go. Maybe this time you'll decide to stay." He drew back and waved them on.

"Keep on this road," Henrietta said. "It's about ten miles."

He drove on more slowly and at a hilltop said, "That is some river, Henri. Some force of nature made it turn right around—" he squinted, looking out across the rich loamy fields, "every time it traveled a few hundred yards."

"You're right, the river is like a snake coiling perpetually."

"It's very pretty."

"It's very beautiful."

"Yes," he said. "Beautiful."

They drove a few more miles. "That"—she pointed to the huge structure they were passing—"is a grain elevator. They store the grain there until it's picked up by the freight trains and taken off to our—to Canadian cities."

"Henri"—Reuben was amused—"you're explaining grain elevators to a North Dakota boy?" Silence once again.

When the road sign for Letellier came into view, Henri said,

"Take that turn. I'll tell you where to go when we get into town."

In a few minutes, passing by sturdy wooden houses and some children having a bicycle race, they reached the driveway Henrietta was looking for. Following her instructions, Reuben pulled in. On the right was a wooden church, feeling its years. Henri opened the car door and walked to the adjacent house, ringing the doorbell. Tieless, dressed in a sport shirt, a bald elderly man, heavyset, opened the door.

"Ma chère Henriette! Entres-y!" They embraced, and then the priest shook hands with Reuben and led them to the living room. He pointed to the seemingly endless array of photographs of young girls at commencement time lining the hallway. "If you look, you can find yourself in the photograph of your class at Saint Joseph's. I'm too nearsighted to make it out, dear Henriette."

"I didn't stay on for graduation, Father. I went back to Paris."

"Oh, yes, I remember now, and how sad the sisters were to see you leave. How is your dear father?"

"He is well. He has a new book out. I brought you a copy. *Les Œuvres d'Auvergne*, it's called."

Father Lully put on his glasses and reached for the book, focusing on the dust jacket. He lapsed into French, and spoke of his last meeting with Raymond Leborcier. "It's been ten years, hasn't it, since he returned to Paris?"

Henri started to reply in French, but then raised her hand. "Reuben doesn't speak French, Father."

"Dommage," the old priest smiled. "Never mind. In Manitoba we missionary priests can certainly manage in English.

Elise, I'm sure, has prepared tea for you—for you both." He called out and a matronly woman came in from the back of the house. She said something quietly in French to the priest, who raised his hand to his neck, confirming the absence of his collar. "I'll be right back."

He soon reappeared, wearing now his clerical collar and a black wool jacket. "Excuse me!" He bowed his head slightly. "J'étais déshabillé. Now, go to the tray and arrange what you want in your tea, and take some cookies. Elise's special oatmeal cookies."

Reuben ate hungrily. Henri nibbled at a cookie and greeted with relief Father Lully's conversational initiative, reminiscences of the periods in her life when they had known each other—first when she was a young girl, up to age eleven, when her mother died. "In Raymond's arms, after receiving the last sacraments, you and I praying in the little hospital room. She was very beautiful, very devoted." And then at age fourteen, when her father sent her back from France to spend a year at the convent school. "Will you go back to France when you graduate from the university?"

Henri said she hadn't decided. "I am studying library science. And of course the protocols I've learned are all in English. I'm not certain I could practice that profession usefully in France."

Reuben interrupted. "Presumably, Henri, they have libraries in France, and there are equivalent French words for whatever it is they are teaching you at Grand Forks." Turning to the priest: "She is very modest, Father, about her accomplishments. She is a *leading* student."

Father Lully looked into the eyes of the engaging young man with the lock of blond hair over his left eye, erect but utterly relaxed, quick with a smile. Reuben was put out that he could not join them in French. "I'm thinking of learning French, Father. Just something I've put off. Other interests, other concerns." Then another of his appealing smiles.

Henrietta took the bit in her teeth. "Yes." Her voice was earnest. "And one of his concerns, Father, as I told you on the phone, is that in seven months he will be a father. I am the mother. And I brought Reuben here because I want you to marry us."

Reuben sprang up, put one hand on the back of the sofa, and stared down at Henri. Then he looked over at the priest, who reached nervously into his pocket, bringing up a pipe.

"*Henri! Are you crazy?*"

"No. If you do not want to raise our child, that's one thing. But he will not be born without a father."

"Of course. Of course." Reuben nodded, distracted, turning his head, as if for relief, to look at the bookshelf.

Father Lully rose. "I will leave you here and go to my study. Call for me when you want me. If you want me. Anything else you want, Elise is here." They could hear the door shut, and then Reuben's arms were around her. Both of them wept.

"This is what you want, darling?"

"It's what I want, and to be with you for the rest of my life."

"You know that will be so—we've talked about that often, our life together. But that was to be life after we graduated from college, no?"

"Yes. But— But, Reuben, I cannot stay on at Grand Forks

after the pregnancy becomes visible. I have decided. I will go to Paris for the spring semester. We will be married now, but that will be *our* secret."

They kissed again. Reuben walked to the end of the room and knocked on the door of the priest's study.

CHAPTER 6

Grand Forks, December 1969

To get a written note from Eric Monsanto was itself something of a rebuke. Why mail a note to a classmate and close collaborator instead of just calling him on the telephone? Besides, Reuben's dorm was exactly five minutes' drive from the house where Rico lived with his family. There had to be a reason for posting a letter. Reuben opened it sensing that it would not be a routine communication.

"I know you have other concerns in life," the letter was typed single-spaced, "like, the welfare of the whole fucking college. But you were elected editor of the *Dakota Student* on the understanding that you'd give the office the time it needs. You were absent from the meeting on Thursday to plan the Friday issue, and absent on Monday from the meeting to plan the Tuesday issue. Maybe you should have been elected business manager instead of editor. Forget that. The business manager couldn't get away with neglecting the paper." It was signed, simply, "Eric."

Reuben showed the note to Henri when he picked her up at the library, where they regularly met at noon, going on to the Memorial Union for lunch. "Hardly the kind of letter one expects from one's best friend."

"Honey, does it occur to you that maybe Rico has a legitimate complaint?"

"Well, sure. But *you* know why I couldn't be at the *Student* on Thursday, don't you?"

"No."

The reproachful tone of her reply warranted reprisal. "Oh, you didn't know? I was busy fixing up a duck blind."

She swatted him lightly on the head with her book. "Eric can fix his own duck blind."

"Hmm. Yes. *Anyway*, dear Henri, the duck blinds are off-limits. Duck-hunting season is still on. No, listen, it wasn't the duck blinds. I've got about the best excuse possible. Thursday was the university trustees' meeting, and I am required to stand by, in case a student-body question comes up. It's a duty of the chairman of the Student Council—that's me, your—"

"My what?"

Reuben's pause was freighted. But then quickly, "Your servant and lover. Who shares a big secret with you."

"Pass the mustard."

"Okay, if you ask me in French."

Henrietta broke into one of her radiant smiles. "Don't make fun of the French language, honey. You'll get onto it."

Reuben had taken a *Living French* record album from the library, promising to practice a half hour every morning before breakfast. That promise was made a month ago, on the solemn drive back from Letellier. Every now and then, though only when he asked her to do so, she would test him on his progress. When he wanted her to drill him, he would always use the identical prompt, the line from the ditty sung by French children of kindergarten age: *Savez-vous planter les choux?*—"Do you know how to plant cabbages?" She would grin, and pursue the drill for fifteen minutes. But today what he wanted was to talk about Eric's note, and this conversation would be in English.

The note had clearly upset him.

"So what are you going to do? Which reminds me—you dodgy old politico—you explained why you couldn't make the Thursday meeting at the *Student*. What about the Monday meeting? Were you picketing the draft board?—Never mind. But you will swear by your wife and child to attend future editorial meetings. Right, Reuben?"

"I promise."

"How'm I going to check on you when I'm in Paris?"

"Don't even mention Paris."

"I don't intend to give birth to our child in the Burtness Theater."

"I know, I know, but let's not go into it. Though you know something? I've been trying to figure out a way to visit you in Paris, maybe during the Easter break."

"Visiting me while I'm living with my father will take, well, a little planning."

It was hard to do what he felt like doing, the student dining hall offering no cozy little corners for private affectionate exchanges; so he reached into his pocket for something to write on, and came up with the note from Eric. He turned it over and wrote on the back: "Je t'adore." He signed it with a flourish, "Reuben Hardwick Castle."

CHAPTER 7

Paris, France, December 1969

Raymond Leborcier had excitedly told Nadine, his housekeeper, that little Henrietta, whom Nadine had known since Henri was eleven years old, had married and conceived a child. "I have not met the young man—the lucky young man—who is her husband. His name is Stephen Durban. But he is not lucky in everything. He has been drafted into the American army and told he will be sent to Hawaii for special training. No doubt he will then be sent on to Vietnam. Dear Henrietta will come here, and have her baby here."

Nadine, a war widow, was instantly sympathetic. She promised to pray daily to her dead husband to solicit special protection for Henrietta's husband. "That terrible Indochina—you do know, Monsieur le professeur, that my Gustave was *almost two full years* fighting for his country—and much good it did, with that phony treaty, dirty beasts, and General de Gaulle. De Gaulle!" Nadine feigned spitting into the wastebasket. "First he betrayed the Vietnamese and now he wants the United States to betray them also!"

"When will the dear child arrive?"

"Next month, Nadine. The baby will come in June. Meanwhile, Henrietta will study at the university. She is a student of library science."

"Will she live here, in our apartment?"

"At first, yes. And as long as she likes. We will make room— for her and the baby—will we not, Nadine?"

"Of course. And I will look after her night and day."

"Perhaps she will want to get her own place, eventually. Nadine, do you know a good...gynecologist?"

"Dr. Hervier is splendid. Even if he did not succeed in saving my child. There is the problem—" she paused.

"What problem?"

"Dr. Hervier was a great patriot in the Algerian struggle. And I learned from Géraldine—my sister, Géraldine, who is also his patient—that he has resolved to return to Algeria to do his duty. That's the language he used—'do my duty for the people we betrayed.' Gustave would have been proud."

Raymond Leborcier lifted a finger to his lips. He did not welcome talk about the politics of betrayal. Or about any politics at all. His interest was in philology. He was engaged, regularly, in spirited academic exercises having to do with the historical development of the French language. He smiled with satisfaction, recalling the paper in which he had taken on the work of Emile Abélard. He remembered with mortification that he had gone so far as to accuse Professor Berthier of being disloyal to the school of Jean Larousse—a silly point in a learned dispute having to do with pronunciation. On the other hand, "I won that one," he mused, looking up at the shelf where the record of the twenty-year exchange was kept. But then he put his own academic concerns to one side. There were things to do before Henrietta arrived. Not least was integrating her into the university in work that would advance her in the field of library science.

Henrietta was her sparkling self, lively, amiable, undemanding. She told her father—aware that Nadine, in the kitchen, could hear everything she said—that she was deeply in love with her husband, "Stephen," but that she was reconciled to the exclusive demands the United States Army would put on him for some time into the future. They had agreed that they would not attempt to communicate by telephone. They would simply write.

The letters from the United States came in regularly, postmarked from Grand Forks, near which, Henrietta told her father, Private Stephen Durban was stationed pending his transfer to Hawaii. Reuben and Henri had agreed that it would be safer to proceed using an alias, guarding against stray references to Reuben Castle, a name prominent in the Grand Forks area. "Stephen Durban, à ton service," Reuben had said to her at the airport, with a courtly bow in continental fashion, the name pronounced "Duhrbahn" in high French accent.

There was nothing remotely like suspicion or incredulity in the Leborcier household. Raymond's attention, once he had seen to it that his daughter was well cared for and was doing satisfactory work at the university, returned to philology.

Henri thought in an early letter to suggest to Reuben on a diplomatic initiative. "Reuben, why don't you make it a point in one letter, in a few weeks, to say something I can read out at the dinner table, as though written during training for combat duty in Saigon? You might say something like this: 'You've told me that Nadine's husband perished in that terrible part of the world trying to defend the honor of France. Well, I honor *him* for his effort.' Something like that. And listen, darling, if you want to write that passage in *French*, it will mean all the more to her. And to me. You were making such fine progress. Speaking of which, is Rico now satisfied with your work for the *Student*? If he is making trouble, tell me and I will have him drafted immediately. Did you know that Calvin Stokes is not only head librarian at UND, but also *chairman of the draft board*? So if anybody is mean to you, I'll have him sent to Vietnam."

By April the intervals between Reuben's letters had increased. His habit had been to write on Mondays and Thursdays—"I do that right after the editorial meeting. I assign myself a letter to you as first priority. Maybe I should publish these letters! Written in—Savez-vous planter les choux?"

She had no letter from him the first week in April, and his letter the second week was oddly strained, the news perfunctory. She heard nothing the third week. She thought to put in a phone call to the *Dakota Student* office—there was no phone in Reuben's dormitory room—but decided against it. She shook her head, wondering what he might be up to. Might he have returned to Zap to welcome the spring? She did not phone, instead concentrating her thoughts on her work at the university.

She took special pleasure first in reading, and finally in fathoming, the points her father had made in his most recent essay in *La Tradition Gauloise*. She found the French languor in linguistic matters sharply different from American vigilance, which sometimes bordered on the hysterical. The contrast was rather appealing, as if the Académie Française felt no obligation to stay current: *Let the non-monastic world concern itself with such matters.* When the Second World War broke out, Henrietta learned with delight, there was not yet an authorized French term for a bomber. "A bomber, Reuben, is the person who pilots the airplane with bombs in it which are then dropped on evil people. If you are pursuing your studies, you'll find—why not?—*bombardier.* Logical…right? But the Académie didn't authorize the use of the word until sometime after the Nazis conquered Paris. Maybe that's why they didn't bomb Paris! On n'avait pas de bombardiers!!! Reuben, honey, I haven't heard from you in two weeks. That makes me not only mad and jealous and furious and vindictive, but also—a little worried."

She fought back again her rogue impulse to pick up the telephone. Instead, she wrote a letter to Eric Monsanto. Only Eric had been told the truth about the reason for Henri's decision to spend the spring semester in France. "Dear Rico, I do wonder. It's been two weeks without any word. Reassure me. He is well?"

CHAPTER 8

Grand Forks, April 1970

"Reub?"

"Yeah. That you, Rico?"

"Yes. And I've got to see you."

"About what?"

"I've got to see you."

Reuben would normally have replied with a jocularity of some sort, but the tone of Eric's voice told him, *Not today*. Well, at least Eric hadn't announced himself in another written note.

Reuben was close to Eric. They had discovered each other as freshmen, the day of the required physical exam. Because the student currently being examined required protracted attention from the doctor, those behind him in line had to wait. Reuben and Eric, half naked, were seated on a bench in the anteroom.

"I'm Reuben. Reuben Castle, from Fargo."

"I'm Eric, Eric Monsanto. My people live here in Grand Forks."

"Why didn't they look after your health?"

Eric laughed. "They don't believe in prophylactics."

"I'll give you some from my personal supply, soon as we get out of here."

Filing past the last medical clerk, Eric looked at his watch. It was two long hours since he had reported for the examination. He looked back. Reuben was just behind, filling out one last form. Eric went out the door of the McCannell Hall Physical Health Center and paused, adjusting his eyes to the bright September sunshine. Reuben emerged.

"You want to have lunch?"

"Sure. I guess that's next door, at the Memorial Union." Reuben pointed. "How come you're only a freshman? You look old and wizened."

Rico Monsanto was dark-haired and suntanned. He hadn't shaved that morning. He smiled at the allusion to his seniority and they set out together for the Commons.

"As a matter of fact, I took a couple of years off after school. I worked on a freighter. Maybe they aged me, the Swedes. I did feel about a thousand years older when I finally peeled away."

"That was just now?"

"No. About a year ago. Then I bummed around some. My father's a lawyer in town. He practically got an injunction to bring me home to begin college."

They reached the cafeteria and stood in line for food. After finishing their lunch and drinking their coffee, they were still conversing. "But after the Tonkin Gulf business my dad—he's a carpenter—thought it was pretty obvious that the war was going to escalate, and he said"—Reuben mimicked a stentorian voice—" 'If you die over there, I want them to know they knocked off an *educated* American.' "

Both laughed. "Well, I've got an advantage over you, besides my extreme old age," Eric said. "This is my hometown, and I can show you around a bit."

Rico became Reuben's confidant. Having competed together for staff membership on the *Dakota Student*, each made his own mark on the paper. Reuben was impulsive, Rico deliberate. Although both aspired to be elected, eventually, editor in chief, Eric acknowledged to himself that Reuben's talents as an entrepreneur exceeded his own—Eric Monsanto would never have come up with the Zap initiative. So he quietly applauded Reuben's success, encouraged him in many of his ventures, and collaborated with him in some. These included the night at the duck blind in September, when Reuben had airily declined to take the advice of his senior counselor. This time it was Reuben who was short of prophylactics.

Eric said he'd pick Reuben up at the *Student* office. At six, Reuben stepped into the familiar 1964 Chevrolet coupé, a high-school graduation present to Eric from his father.

"Where we going, Rico?"

"I figured to get supper at the Hop See."

"Always good. You going to eat out my ass over something?"

"Yes."

Reuben's apprehension heightened when Eric ordered iced tea. All the more reason, Reuben calculated, to go in the other direction. He ordered a double daiquiri. To the familiar waiter he said, "Joe, you got some Myers rum?"

The drinks came.

"Okay," Eric said. "You didn't want the baby. But she said no when you suggested an abortion. You told me you talked with her about who would take care of the baby after it was born; you suggested she give it up for adoption. But she wouldn't agree to that either. She didn't want to stick around once the pregnancy showed, and on that point she took the initiative, went off to Paris. You talked about how the two of you would live—"

"You're the only one who knows all this, Rico."

"Yes. I'm not going to publish it in the *Student*. And I bet I'm also the only one who knows—besides you—that you haven't written a letter to her in three weeks."

There was a drop in Reuben's composure. "Yeah. She told you, I guess."

"Yes. Look, if you're thinking of leaving her, you can't go about it this way, just *not writing her*. Have you decided to walk out on her?"

Reuben lowered his head. He took a long swallow of his drink. Then looked up. "Yes. Yes, Rico. I don't want to be married and have a child at age twenty-one."

Eric came close to giving his thoughts free rein. It flashed through his mind to get up from the table, get into his car, and drive off. He was deterred by the graphic mental picture of his sometime best friend, the young, blue-eyed Student Council chairman who still looked like a student cheerleader, left standing outside the rustic motel/bar/brothel without even transportation for the ten miles back to his dormitory. The son of a bitch, he thinks only of Reuben Castle, Rico thought. But finally he rejected the idea of leaving him stranded. He asked only, "Reuben. Are you absolutely decided on this?"

"Yes," Reuben nodded. "And I guess I'd want you to know it wasn't easy."

Eric could bring himself to say only this much: "Then you have to write and tell her. Tell her right away."

Reuben nodded. "Yes. And if you don't want to see me again, I'll understand."

"I'll decide about that." He rose to pay the bill. "Sometime."

CHAPTER 9

Paris, May 1970

Professor Leborcier had gone to Lyon for a meeting of the French Academy of Philology and would be away until Friday. Henri was told firmly by Nadine that suppers would routinely be prepared for her, and that she, Nadine, would be distressed if Henri made plans to eat out. "There is no reason for you to go out to a restaurant, and there are good reasons not to move about the city more than you have to in your condition."

"What's wrong with my condition?" Henri smiled mockingly, looking over the day's mail on the tray. She reached out for the letter with her name and address handwritten, the envelope bearing an American stamp. "But, Nadine, you are always so kind. All I need is soup and a piece of bread."

"And a glass of wine. I have a Château Raspail that has just come in. They are practically giving it away, at sixteen francs."

But Henri was no longer listening. She had slipped into the living room and turned on the lamp on her father's desk.

When, a half hour later, Nadine called her to the dining room, Henri's face was white.

"You are unwell, my little girl?"

"No. I'm fine. But I'm not hungry." She reached for a piece of bread to appease Nadine. "I will take this upstairs. I have some reading to do."

It was just after midnight that Nadine heard the cry. She opened her door and rushed up the stairs to Henri's bedroom. Another cry came as she opened the door. "Nadine, Nadine! The baby is coming!"

Nadine flew out the door. "I have Dr. Hervier's home telephone number." She was back in the bedroom in moments. "I rang and rang and rang. No answer. I think, chère Henri, I will get an ambulance to take you to Saint-Jean."

Nadine was gone again to the telephone. Henri closed her eyes and let out another cry of pain.

Twenty minutes later the ambulance was there. A half hour after Henri arrived at the hospital, the baby was born, a month before he was due. Nadine was not back in the apartment until four in the morning. She had telephoned Raymond Leborcier from the hospital but had to settle for leaving a message with the desk clerk. "Tell Professor Leborcier," she said excitedly, "that he gave birth to—I mean, his daughter gave birth to a little boy. The baby is a month premature but doing well. The professor can call me when he gets this message. Mademoiselle—*Madame* Durban is at the Saint-Jean hospital, 524.43.64. But it would be better not to disturb her. Monsieur le professeur can call me instead. The number is—" She was excited, but stopped herself before giving to the desk clerk, to hand on to Professor Leborcier, the telephone number of Professor Leborcier.

Returned to the apartment, she paused to draw breath. She thought to look into Henri's bedroom before going to bed herself—there might be bedclothes that needed to be taken away. She looked at the night table, switching on the light. There was only a ripped-open envelope and a letter. She looked at it curiously. It didn't bear the handwriting she had gotten used to, or the return address of "Private Durban." On the envelope, in the sender's corner, was written, simply, "Monsanto." The stationery was that of "*Dakota Student*, University of North Dakota, Grand Forks, N.D." Nadine's knowledge of English was insecure, but curiosity drove her to make an attempt to decipher the opening lines. They read: "*I cannot bear to give you this terrible news. When you wrote . . .*"

"Terrible news"? Nadine did not have the heart to grapple with the lines that ensued. A wise Frenchwoman with experience in life and in tragedy, she knew what it must mean, this "terrible news." It could only mean that Stephen Durban, the husband of Henrietta and the father of her child, had been killed. It was the shock of getting that news that had brought on the premature birth of the baby.

Beyond telling the professor what had happened, Nadine reflected, *she must not let on that she knew what the letter said*. Not let on to Henrietta, or anybody else. Possibly—she gave ground here to her conscience—she would tell her mother when she visited her on Sunday. Chère Maman was very old, and would not breathe a word of it, not even to her priest, the holy Père Toussaint.

BOOK TWO

CHAPTER 10

Boulder, Colorado, February 1987

"Did I tell you I'm on the committee for Thursday evening's speech?" Amy asked.

"Which speech?" Henri replied. "There are usually six speeches you can choose from. My goodness, *everybody* comes to Boulder."

The boy's young voice interrupted. "Not *everybody*, Maman. *Presque* tout le monde."

In the small, comfortable apartment, Henrietta looked over at her sixteen-year-old son. Her vision blurred. She was seeing Reuben Castle. That's how old Reuben was—sixteen—when she first laid eyes on him at the Memorial Union in Grand Forks, in 1966. They were both freshmen at the University of North Dakota. But no—Reuben had been older than Justin now was, surely? She closed her eyes to do the arithmetic.

—Reuben was born in August 1948.

—Therefore, in September 1966 he was eighteen years old. Not sixteen, Justin's age.

"Justin, I have told you not to speak in French except when we are alone."

Amy interceded. "Oh, come on, Henrietta. It's good for *me* when he speaks in French. And what he said wasn't very difficult to understand."

"That's right, Mrs. Parrish." Justin got up from his chair and pulled from the bookcase his watercolor set. He wiped off the brush before continuing. "But it *was* difficult to understand why Maman said that *everybody* comes to Boulder. Do you know, Mrs. Parrish, about the three men in the train who passed the cow? The brown cow?"

Amy reconciled herself to hearing again what the students had been told in Mr. Edwards's trigonometry class at school. She smiled at Henri over her coffee cup—she understood. She too had a teenage boy.

"No, tell me about the cow, Justin."

"Well, when they passed the cow, the economist said, 'It appears that the cows in Ireland are brown.' The mathematician said, 'No, John, all you are able to say is that *some* of the cows in Ireland are brown.'"

Justin paused, permitting his mother's guest, the lively middle-aged woman, head of the special-collections division of the Chinook Library, to absorb the lesson thus far. Then he dipped his hand into his pocket and brought out a pair of glasses.

Donning them, he arched his eyebrows and spoke in deep, authoritative tones: "'No, Rudolph'—this is the logician speaking, Mrs. Parrish—'you are entitled to say only this, *We know that in Ireland there is at least one cow, of which at least one side is brown.'*"

Justin broke into a smile of boyish pleasure. "You like that, Mrs. Parrish?"

She replied, teasingly, "Je l'aime beaucoup, Justin."

He went back to his watercolors. "I've got to go to the paint store soon, Maman."

"Well, you know where it is, Justin. On your bicycle it will take you...not more than twelve minutes."

"Oh. I thought you might want to drive me."

"No. What you thought was: *There is a driver. There is a car. So I can be driven to the store.* Me, I thought: *There is a bicycle and a store, and only one brown cow who has a driver's license.*"

"Mrs. Parrish," Justin turned to her, a little indignantly, "your Allan has a driver's license, and he's only three months older than I am."

"Justin, I am not here as a family broker on the question of a driver's license."

Henrietta broke in, addressing a few words in French to her son. To Amy she said that she wanted to wait for the doctor's analysis of Justin's eye problems—"He only started wearing glasses a month ago."

"And I don't really need them, Maman. Only when I'm looking in dictionaries, that kind of thing. Not when I'd be driving a car."

Amy Parrish accepted another cup of coffee and returned to the subject of the evening speech. "It's sponsored by the Boulder Democratic Caucus. Come to think of it, Henrietta, I don't even know whether you're a Democrat! I simply assumed you were. Everybody who's educated is."

From Justin: "President Reagan is not a Democrat, and he's educated."

Amy thought to be cautious. "Well, there are two views on that subject, Justin. But Henrietta, dear, I'm trying to find out whether you'd like to come with me to the talk. Obviously you don't have to contribute anything."

"Who's the speaker?"

"Senator Reuben Castle. North Dakota. He's supposed to be very good."

"*Supposed to be.* . . . How many people is that, Mrs. Parrish, when you're *supposed* to be good? Like one thousand think you're good? Like one million?"

Henrietta Durban rose from her chair. Amy noticed that her face was pale. "You all right, Henri?"

"I'll be right back."

She was gone five minutes. When she came back her color had returned, and she took up the conversation where they had left off.

"Where are you sitting, Amy?"

"Thursday night? I'm on the committee, so I can sit wherever I want. Would you like to sit onstage? There'll be a lot of people onstage, including our mayor and our governor—at least, the governor promised to come."

"I have a lot to do. If I go, I'll probably get there late. I'd better sit in the back."

"Can I go too?" Justin asked.

"Yes," his mother said. "You can come with me."

When, soon after her father's death, Henrietta Leborcier Durban accepted the offer from the University of Colorado library, she and her son, just turned fifteen, settled into an apartment near the campus. No one, not even Amy Parrish, her superior at the library, questioned her closely on her marriage or on the circumstances of the death in Vietnam of her husband, Lieutenant Durban. Henrietta didn't bring up the subject; nor did Justin, who had been told as a little boy that his father had died in military service, and that this was why he was fatherless.

CHAPTER 11

Boulder, February 1987

Looking around, Henri estimated that several hundred people were at the Democratic rally in Macky Auditorium. The meeting had begun, or so it had been advertised, at seven-fifteen. Henri arrived with Justin at about seven-thirty. She led him to a seat just in front of the last row, where a half dozen girls were waiting to hoist placards designed to stimulate Democratic passions. As Henri and Justin took their seats, the welcoming speaker was pronouncing a litany of the evil deeds of the Reagan administration. When he was done, the canned music blared in. The apogee—as always—was "Happy Days Are Here Again." That melody evoked the sacred historical memory of Franklin Delano Roosevelt. In 1932 he had mesmerized the convention in Chicago and, four months later, the voting public nationwide in his decisive victory over President Herbert Hoover—the "Prince of Depression." Tonight's speaker in Boulder had referred to Mr. Hoover using the same words, perhaps the millionth time he had been thus recalled to the memory of Democratic audiences. The speaker waved his hands voluptuously as the music played, jubilant music, happiness-is-ahead-for-us music.

It was several minutes before the Democratic congressman

was introduced, an elderly man who looked lean and hungry and who was very very indignant about everything President Reagan had done, touching on Iran, Nicaragua, and Ollie North.

"But you're not here tonight," Congressman Atkins said, addressing the house full of Democrats, half of them students, "to rue yesterday's political news. You're here to celebrate *tomorrow's* political news." Henri found herself gripping the wrist of Justin, who was carried away by the proceedings, clapping boisterously whenever the audience gave him a lead with its applause. "You're here to listen to a young shining star in the Democratic pantheon." Atkins paused theatrically.

"Now let me tell you about Reuben Hardwick Castle. Going back not that long—just fifteen, twenty years—he was the most prominent member of his class at the University of North Dakota. Editor in chief of the student newspaper, chairman of the Student Council. He was brave in denouncing the war, but he refused to shield himself from it. He even put off law school, waiting till after his military service to begin law studies at the University of Illinois, all of this so that he could do what he thought was his duty." The applause had been dutiful, but now was proud.

"He was, fortunately, spared the bloody end so many members of his generation suffered in that terrible war under the leadership of President Nixon. He returned home safely, entering law school the following September. But he didn't complete his studies—in good conscience he *couldn't* complete his studies while he saw the terrible shape his country was in. He was drawn to public life, to do what any good citizen would do—put his God-given talents to work in order to serve his country." There was a ripple of applause.

"Hold your applause, please, ladies and gentlemen, gathered in this hall of this distinguished university—it gets better. When he was out here in Colorado on a speaking tour for the Democratic Party, he met and soon afterward married a young lady who had been Miss *Colorado*—and then had gone on to become Miss *America*!" There was substantial applause.

"Elle est ici?" Justin whispered to his mother.

"On ne sait pas, Justin."

"Je voudrais la voir."

"On verra." They would soon know whether Mrs. Castle was there.

"Priscilla Castle is the mother of a fine young man, and if he's lucky, one day in just a few years he'll be a student at the University of Colorado—" There was enthusiastic applause. "And if he *does* enter this university, I know he'll end up a proud member of the Democratic Caucus." The applause now was sustained.

"Reuben Castle was elected first as North Dakota's sole member of the House of Representatives, where I am honored to serve as one of Colorado's proud delegation." The applause had now thinned out. "Only six years ago, he was elected to the Senate, replacing a long-serving Republican. He easily won re-election last fall.

"So! I'm delighted tonight to introduce this great young Democrat. And just to show the special esteem he has for the University of Colorado"—the speaker was slowing down the words he spoke and augmenting the volume with which he spoke them—"he has brought with him *Miss America*—she is *still* that, always Miss America, as far as the citizens of Colorado are concerned!"

The congressman turned on his heel and gestured to the people seated on the stage behind him.

Justin felt the sudden pressure of his mother's hand. "Qu'est-ce que c'est, Maman?"

"*Nothing. Quiet.*" Her eyes were fixed on the stage. *Had she spoken too sharply to her son?* She would make up for it.

"Quiet, darling," she said, her tone softened.

CHAPTER 12

Boulder, February 1987

Amy dropped her handwritten letter off at Henri's apartment early the next morning. The envelope was marked: *En route to Aspen, skiing.* The lettering on the envelope was large and distinctive.

The missive read, "Glad you came last night! I spotted you, and hoped to catch you afterward, but you had already left. I think Senator Castle is quite smashing, and who knows, we may all be hearing from him from a higher platform in a year or so. And Priscilla's—well, I've known her since she was sixteen. I almost wrote sexteen. Enough said.

"I mean, enough said on *that*. Henri, I've known you nearly two years now, so I'm going to give you some advice. Big-sister advice, since I'm a dozen years older than you. It boils down to: Get around a bit. This campus is, well, maybe not *teeming* with attractive disengaged males, but there are some nice people here. They may not be in the same league as your Mr. Durban (sorry, I've never known his first name), but.... Well. How many years since he died? I guess as many years as Justin is old, if I work it out right. Justin is divine, but you can't very well cohabit with him and anybody else at the same time.

"I warned you early on about my reputation. J. is a junior

now, one year behind my Allan. You can't send him away yet, not for a while, but at college time, he should certainly go away. Leaving you with a little privacy. Don't be sore at me for poking into other people's business. How can anybody *help* other people *without* getting into their business? You can always tell me to shove off, but I don't think you will. And I don't think you should."

Henrietta walked into the kitchen, Amy's letter folded in her pocket. Justin was eating his cereal absentmindedly, his eyes on the television screen. Henri looked up. The caption on the Sony read, "Senator Reuben Castle speaking at Democratic rally." The camera zoomed back and showed Priscilla Castle, gazing devotedly at her husband. Seated next to her was their son, who looked to be about eleven. He was wholly detached from the scene. His jacket and shirt seemed to grow larger as the seconds ticked on, but it was an illusion, as the boy wearing them mentally distanced himself, shrinking from the proceedings. But when the crowd broke out in applause and the boy's eyes moved toward his father, Mrs. Castle could be seen discreetly nudging him.

The television commentator took over. "Senator Castle, with his family looking on, complained about the policies of President Ronald Reagan at a meeting sponsored by the Democratic Caucus of the University of Colorado. He was well received, and there is talk that Democrats might find his name on the national ticket, if not next year, then perhaps in 1992."

The television image gave way to a commercial.

"Maman? Il est bien fort, ce monsieur, non?"

"Yes. He's very attractive, and very impressive. Justin, have you thought of going away over spring break?"

"You mean to Paris?"

"No. I was thinking of a skiing vacation. Your friend Charley is always talking about skiing vacations. And Mrs. Parrish says that Alta, in Utah, where Allan goes, is very nice, and not expensive."

Justin pushed his cereal bowl away. "Are *you* going to take a vacation?"

"I hadn't planned to."

"Do colleges have vacations? I mean, for college employees? I mean, do you get paid if you take a vacation?"

"There are rules and accommodations. The library doesn't close down, in the way—well, in the way the dining halls more or less close down. The library stays open."

"So you *can't* take a vacation."

"I can. Tais-toi. I'm talking about *you* having a vacation. Without your mother."

"Gee. That could be fun!"

She feigned annoyance, batting him on the head with a paper napkin, and reminding herself, for the twentieth time since Tuesday, that Justin was only two years younger than Reuben Castle had been when that dreamy young freshman entered her life.

CHAPTER 13

Washington, D.C., March 1987

Priscilla Avery Castle put down the phone. She sat still for a moment. Then she moved her chair two inches to the left, so that she could look squarely into the mirror.

She didn't like to look at herself at an angle, even at the very slight angle that permitted her to cradle the telephone in her dressing room. Angles create distortions, more distortions than the ones she had no alternative but to submit to: fourteen years of aging, not entirely hidden by cosmetics and surgery. That was distortion enough—she moved her head back a bit, and looked into the mirror. But then, quickly, she lowered her chin. If the head is back too far, the nostrils are exposed to unflattering attention. She remembered her coach, back in Denver. "*Never permit the camera to look into your nose!*" Amos made his point: "Icky things happen in your nostrils. Ava Gardner's nostrils flare down, so there isn't anything there anybody can look at, except a nose. You don't have a nose built that way, Prissy. So don't expose it.

"Oh, yes," Amos had gone on. "And work with your boobs. I don't mean shove them in everybody's face. Just watch how you dress. Then they'll claim the right attention without any more help. And remember, *everything* has to be there for the camera to look at. It's the composite picture. That's the word, composite."

Amos. He was a character, but he knew about fashion and fashion photography—and about beauty contests. They were a sideline, but his name had been associated with the winners of statewide contests in eight of the ten years before Priscilla Avery met him. Always he had hoped for the big prize, the great prize, the only prize. Miss America. Well, she had given him that. Priscilla didn't spend much time saying thanks, but she did have a pleasant thought about Amos.

Bert Whitman, full-time publicist for the state of Colorado, spent half his life in Los Angeles, and that's where he ran into Hank Blokofski, who told him about Amos. Bert was at the Beverly Hills Health Club, up from a swim, lying face down for a massage. Hank Blokofski was doing the same, off to one side. He had concluded a distribution deal after a long, sweaty afternoon session, and had gone over to his health club to relax.

Blokofski had nominally retired from the movie business, but he was a library of knowledge about everything that touched on commercial glamour. In 1970 he had served as a judge in the Miss America contest in Atlantic City. He liked to remember the expression on the face of Nancy Gutierrez when she was transubstantiated from Miss Texas to Miss America. "She seemed such a tender, innocent Texas lady," he reported to friends and associates, and he said it now to Bert, in from Denver. "In fact, Nancy was tougher than a hand iron. But when I spotted her I said to myself, *Go, go, Bloky—go, go, go*, and pretty soon I had the majority of the judges with me."

"What kind of thing do the winners have to do? I mean, other than be beautiful and all that stuff. And maybe screw the judges."

Blokofski ignored the gibe. "There are lots of things. But the A-number-one thing is *never* to have a bad photo, never. And that takes a personal coach. A real expert who coaches professional models and knows the ropes."

"You know some of these...specialists?"

"Oh, sure. For instance, I know Amos Cohen, from your neck of the woods. He narrowly missed in 1968, with a gal from New Mexico. But he's a real pro."

Whitman, with his eye out for the commerce he was professionally engaged in stimulating, moved quickly. As soon as he returned to Denver he requisitioned photos of the contestants for Miss Colorado. He picked out Priscilla Avery. He telephoned her, and liked what he heard. He even found pleasing her hint of a southern accent, left over, she told him, from her childhood in Alabama. Then he called Amos Cohen and invited him to his Chamber of Commerce office, in the great Republic Plaza skyscraper on Seventeenth Street.

"Are you available to handle a Miss America lady?"

"If I think she has a chance."

Bert showed him two photographs.

Amos looked hard at them. And then, "I'd have to meet her."

"Of course. What does it take?"

"You mean for an exclusive?"

"Yes."

"I said I'd have to see her."

"I know you said that. Obviously if you think she hasn't a pig's chance, you'd say no. At least, I hope you would."

"I'd want thirty-five plus expenses. Plus ten if she makes it to Miss Colorado. Plus fifty if she makes it to Miss America. And expenses. That includes a couple of hot dogs for cooperative photographers and other nice people."

"Well, the next step is you interview Priscilla Avery."

"And your next step, Mr. Whitman, is to make a commitment."

"If you say it's a go at your end, I think—I said I *think*—I can manage your fee with the Chamber of Commerce. I'll tell them that to get a Miss America will be worth a billion dollars to Colorado."

"That's a good safe figure."

"You won't have any trouble getting through to Priscilla." He passed over the photographs. "Give me a call when you've talked to her."

"When I've *seen* her."

"Yep. Maybe by the end of the week?"

"Maybe. I'll call you."

CHAPTER 14

Washington, D.C./Aiken, South Carolina, March 1987

"Does Castle like golf?"

"Sure."

"Why don't we make it then for next month, look in at the Masters? Everybody goes there, nobody is really conspicuous."

"I'll check it out with him," said Susan, chief aide to Senator Castle. "His calendar is clear for that weekend. He would probably need—I mean, it would make sense—to have an invitation. Senator Castle doesn't like to do things that can be thought pure self-indulgence. He should be, in some way, part of the show."

"Good. If you have any trouble getting a personal invitation, I know one or two of the pros. 'Dear Senator Castle: I know that you like our sport—*the* sport! I would be honored if you came to the Masters and were there when, I hope, I finally get that green jacket. If you find you can work it into your schedule, I would love to have you as my guest.' Signed, 'Your fan, Hank Wright.' "

"Sounds good." Susan was taking notes, in her fabled shorthand. Nobody, she had boasted at age twenty-two, could speak more rapidly than she could take it down. She winced when reminded, as occasionally happened, that she had once made this claim. Vainglory. Not because it had ceased to be true—her fluency on her notepad was dazzling—but because to say what she had said smacked of, well, exhibitionism.

In her twenties she had developed into a secretary and confidante utterly free of self-concern. She was the secretary about whose private life nothing was known and, after a while, nothing was asked. When, on the death of Congressman Adam Benjamin Jr., she was approached by the personnel hand Howell Anderson and asked to sign up with the newly elected senator from North Dakota, she deliberated the proposal. She was fifty years old, and liked the prospect of a prolonged attachment. It didn't surprise Anderson when she said she would look into Senator Castle's background and only then decide.

While it didn't surprise Anderson that Susan Oakeshott would want to think it over, he *was* surprised that she didn't ask him for the substantial packet of information about Reuben Castle that had been accumulated for the campaign. "Thanks very much, but I can put my hands on everything I'll need to consider."

"Reuben," Anderson had said to him, "it just doesn't matter what the strain on you may be of waiting to organize your office. If she says yes, then you'll have the best office manager in Washington, D.C."

She did say yes. And now, six years later, it was Susan Oakeshott, not the senator, who was approached about an utterly secret meeting between Castle and the quiet kingmaker, Harold Kaltenbach.

What Kaltenbach wanted to deliberate was whether Castle

would make a good presidential candidate five years down the line. "The Republicans are going to take the White House in 1988," he told Susan. "I'm deciding who to back for 1992."

Whom Harold Kaltenbach would back in 1992 was a matter of critical importance to the contending parties. Kaltenbach was from Nebraska. He loved politics, and politics loved him. He loved his money and his network of friends, and he was doggedly attached to the Democratic Party. Susan, of course, knew all this, knew all about Kaltenbach, and she knew that her senator would appreciate the importance of meeting with him as a petitioner, and would agree to have such a meeting on Kaltenbach's terms.

By noon the next day Susan had cleared the Augusta weekend. Working at his end, Kaltenbach had managed an invitation from Hank Wright. The senator would be, unofficially, Wright's guest at Augusta, and would attend as much of the tournament as he could. Kaltenbach would decide—there was plenty of time; the tournament was four weeks off—whether it would be useful to have the senator say a word or two at any of the official functions.

Their actual meeting would be at a golf course—but not the Augusta National. Instead, they would go to nearby Aiken. Kaltenbach and the senator would both be dressed as golfers. Susan had made a reservation at the club dining room in the name of Hank Wright.

The table was at a well-removed corner of the dining room, and they met at eleven-thirty, a half hour before many other patrons would gather.

Harold Kaltenbach was very quiet, embarked on his supercharged mission. Reuben was acutely aware that he was being examined through the special microscope of a true political professional. The questioning was deceptively orthodox: name, rank, and serial number, like a form for a bank loan.

Reuben found his doughty self-confidence strangely useless. He knew that anything that smacked of rodomontade would be...silly. Maybe even fatal. A demonstration of confidence in his political future was of course useful, but it mustn't be superficial. If Reuben Castle was going to talk persuasively about his strengths, he could do so plausibly only by communicating strengths that were not obviously visible to Harold Kaltenbach. But what *wasn't* visible to Harold Kaltenbach? And would the impression be damaging if Reuben miscalculated?

Probably the thing to do was to act absolutely natural. He had this difficulty, which many first-rate politicians caught up in the theater of politics have, namely that he wasn't sure what was in fact natural. Reuben knew that he was attractive to men, even charming; and he could not remember a time when he had failed at ingratiation with women, communally and individually. He had those advantages at the outset.

He braced himself for two questions. How was it that, in fifteen months in Vietnam, he had avoided combat entirely? (He had a pretty satisfactory answer to that one, he thought—he didn't control the combat assignments, after all.) And the second: Why was it that he hadn't finished law school? Complying with the Buckley Amendment of 1974, college administrators were required to make available to students or ex-students any official reports written about them or their work. And ex-students could requisition these, in later years, removing them from the university's files. Why had Reuben done exactly that with his professors' reports from the University of Illinois?

He had an answer, but he knew it wasn't always effective. Garry Givern, a fellow contestant for the Democratic senatorial nomination in 1980, had touched on the delicate point at a party caucus in Bismarck, North Dakota's capital. "Reuben," Givern said, "I pulled out my academic records too. The difference between us is that I am delighted to show mine to anyone who is interested."

Susan had told Reuben that Harold Kaltenbach probably knew about these early exchanges. "He's that kind of man, and he loves it. He could probably sit down tomorrow and do a mini-biography of you."

Reuben had asked, "How many political biographies does he master?"

"Not many. And Lord knows, he doesn't always end up with a winner. But he won't back anybody he thinks has no prospects."

Well, Reuben would soon find out if his answer to the grades-in-law-school question—that the records had been mislaid—was serviceable.

"So, Senator, you decided to go to law school—"

"Please call me Reuben, Mr. Kaltenbach."

"Perhaps in the future. For the time being, if you don't mind, I'll call you 'Senator.' "

Reuben did not surprise himself when he replied, "Whatever you say, Mr. Kaltenbach."

CHAPTER 15

Augusta, Georgia, April 1987

On Saturday, Reuben went out to the golf course with Bill Rode, his young but experienced aide. Rode had arrived in Augusta the night before with a heavy briefcase of work, including drafts of pending legislative bills.

Rode was indispensable to Reuben Castle. He was obsequious and hard-boiled, angular, narrow of frame, and almost always slightly stooped, suggesting a lifetime commitment to subordinate status. His hair was cropped close, and his metal-rimmed glasses fitted tightly. Even at age twenty-six he was wholly lacking in youthful charm, with the result that he achieved his romantic satisfactions secondhand, tilling Senator Castle's discarded territory as best he could.

Today, Rode very much needed from the senator decisions on the proposed special commission charged with reviewing executive authority in foreign policy.

The issue had been raised a month ago by the president. He had let slip (though Reagan-watchers suspected that Reagan hadn't acted unintentionally) a direct challenge to the Boland Amendment, which outlawed material aid to the Nicaraguan contras. When questioned on the subject at his press conference, President Reagan had smiled affably, saying only that it

WILLIAM F. BUCKLEY JR.

would not be right for him, as president, to acquiesce without comment in congressional acts that gainsaid executive prerogatives. "Next question?"

There had been a sustained effort by several reporters to press hard on what had been said. Did President Reagan mean that he did not intend to abide by the terms of the Boland Amendment? Did he have in mind a constitutional adjudication?

"Reagan didn't want to talk about the substantive matter," Rode recalled, as they drove to the National course.

Mr. Reagan's powers to deflect unwelcome questions were highly developed. "When his back is against the wall," Reuben commented, "Reagan resorts to amplification after amplification—did you read the transcript yesterday? He manages to edge himself over to one side of the argument. Then edge himself still farther."

Rode nodded. "And—yes, I did read the text—he concluded with a homily that was simply unrelated to the meaty question of the executive—"

"—overplaying its hand. I don't look forward to the special commission that's going to review the whole question, but I'm willing to serve on it."

"Here's the matter I need to brief you on. Marlin Fitzwater made the president's point later in the afternoon. If Congress nips and tucks at consequences of presidential action, he said, Congress could end up simply aborting antecedent presidential decisions. Mr. Fitzwater gave the example of the Javits Amendment—"

"You mean on supplemental aid to South Vietnam?"

"Yes. The effect of that legislation, Fitzwater said, was to tie the hands of the executive when Nixon attempted to enforce the terms of the Paris cease-fire agreement. I have Fitzwater's statement here," he said, tapping a manila folder on the seat between him and Castle. "This, boss, is what you need to prepare yourself to cope with."

Reuben opened the folder and homed in on the passage marked in red. He read out loud: " 'The cease-fire of January 1973 effectively ended American participation in the Indochina enterprise, with the return of U.S. troops starting almost immediately. The president feels that the question is overdue for exploration whether Congress can retroactively usurp the president's authority in foreign affairs by denying him authority to conclude arrangements he had made without any challenge to their constitutionality.'

"Well. I certainly challenged their constitutionality."

"Yes, I know. But the point, as raised by Reagan, is something we—you—haven't dealt with. The question of ex post facto repeal of presidential foreign policy."

Oh, my, Reuben thought, hemmed in with his aide in the front seat. Dear Bill can go on and on.

Reuben didn't answer directly, but he thought deeply on the point. The name of Senator Castle was actively invoked in the controversy, given the speeches he had made for a number of years challenging the legal authority for the Vietnam War. As an activist on the question, Reuben wasn't surprised that he had not been named by the president to serve on the commission, but it was widely acknowledged that he was nevertheless a prominent spokesman for the case for defining (in this case, trimming) presidential authority.

Reuben looked out the window. Bill Rode, at the wheel, was

inching the car forward at five miles per hour. They were part of the long caravan of automobiles and buses transporting enthusiasts to the links. "By the way, does Hank Wright have any chance of winning?"

"He's very hot. He finished the second round two under par, behind only Larry Mize and Greg Norman. I assume you want us to claw our way to wherever he's playing. It's the third round today. There are four golf theaters going on simultaneously."

"Yeah, that would be nice, Bill, to go to where our host is playing. Nice thinking. You have good political instincts."

"I'm learning from you." The twenty-six-year-old, who had been an honors student in political science at the University of Virginia, attempted a smile.

"Well, Bill, if you're training as a politician, answer me this one: am I wise to just leave it that with Edmund Muskie on the panel, I'm satisfied that our views will be adequately represented? Or should I make a scene and say that our position is underrepresented, since Muskie is only one of five members of the proposed panel?"

I'll be goddamned, Rode said to himself. Rode was not backward as a political analyst. *Our boy is thinking 1992!* "Well, I'd say—I'd suggest—that you just say at your next press conference that you have great respect for Mr. Muskie, and you know he will represent well the views of those who oppose unconstitutional arrogations of power by the chief executive." He paused with his single quite captivating expression, in which he managed to combine official skepticism and scarcely concealed derision.

Reuben smiled in return. "I'll have to go to the party tonight. But after lunch, let's go to my room and review the material you brought."

"Sure. Yes, sir."

Late in the afternoon Susan reached him. "Are you alone, Senator?"

"Yes, Susan. Bill went up to his own room, so he could watch the rest of the match on television. You got news?"

"Yes, I do. You passed the first test with Harold Kaltenbach. With him, as maybe I told you, the meetings and interrogations go through stages. In the first, he passes judgment on whether your appearance and style can go big-time."

"So, I made it through stage one?"

"Yes. He's ready now for stage two. That entails, I know from a couple of survivors, pretty intimate interrogation, the kind of thing you'd expect if you were applying to the FBI or the CIA. What it comes down to, really, is a search for anything the opposition could go to town with. He wants to set up that kind of meeting with you."

"You said yes, I'd agree to that. Obviously."

"Obviously. But he's not quite ready. He wants to do more of his own reading over the weekend. He asked for a date on Monday. Your calendar is clean, but you can't be spotted in his company. You know that; we've discussed it. He has a friend—hell, he has a friend everywhere—he has a friend who keeps a boat on the Potomac. He said, 'What about ten A.M. aboard the *Circe*?'"

"Are you sure the *Circe* isn't a Soviet spy ship?"

WILLIAM F. BUCKLEY JR.

"No, Senator." Susan laughed. "But I'll investigate before you meet him there. Are you saying yes?"

"Yes, Susan. I mean, I want to be president, and this seems to be what I have to go through to get there. Susan, do you agree with me?"

"That you should want to be president?"

He laughed, "Okay, go with it," and hung up the phone.

It rang seconds later. It was Bill Rode. "Senator, get this! Hank Wright is tied for the lead with Larry Mize! There'll be a lot of excitement going into the final round tomorrow. Want me to leave your congratulations at his HQ?"

"Yeah, do that."

"You need anything in the meantime?"

"Nothing much. Maybe some pussy."

CHAPTER 16

Augusta, April 1987

It was indeed a boisterous party. Under the white plastic tent, drinks flowed freely. The dusk was kept at bay with electric chandeliers overhead, and hurricane lamps on white-clad tables. Tired golfers mingled, their thoughts elsewhere, as VIPs bumped shoulders with young southern talent in skintight dresses. Hank Wright made an appearance. Unsurprisingly, he had nothing to drink, except the glass of dark brown liquid in his hand, and no one expected to learn from him whether that was Coca-Cola or Pepsi Cola. He would not risk affronting either of the giants on the eve of the critical round. If he won it, his managers could turn either to Coke or to Pepsi for future sponsorship.

That didn't discourage anybody else. There were a hundred people crowded into the tent—family, sponsors, friends, celebrities. There was a special exultancy among the friends of Hank Wright and Larry Mize. Which of them would be festive twenty-four hours later depended on how those two players, and the two or three others within striking distance, performed the next day. But one of the two was likely to emerge as champion. That called for another drink.

The bartender had his own quickie version of a mint julep.

Never mind. It was nearly as good as the real thing, Lucille said. Lucille was the principal hostess, in charge of welcoming the guests and directing them to the bar, and going back and forth to the console to increase the volume of the canned music or to decrease it. By seven o'clock it needed to be loud because everybody was speaking at the top of his lungs, just to be heard.

With the rich curves of a twenty-year-old and the confidence of twice that age, Lucille made her way through the crowd, her auburn curls bobbing slightly, her scarlet gown parting the gray, beige, blue. To be greeted by Lucille was to be assured a pleasant welcome.

Lucille had intended to welcome Senator Castle as simply one more VIP, pausing, as she did with other prominent guests, to chat for a minute or two before going back to the entrance to look after latecomers.

But she found she didn't want to leave this alluring young senator. There were, to begin with, his striking looks, and the appealing cock to his head as he leaned forward struggling to make out what you were saying. "You have to try one of Ernie's mint juleps, Senator." She spoke in Deep South. "He's famous for them. Can I bring you one?"

"Why not? But"—he extended his hand to the sleeve of her dress—"not if it means I'm going to lose you."

"That won' happen, Senator. I promise you that."

And it didn't happen. She was back in moments with a mint julep for him and, for herself, a cola.

"You didn't tell me what to call you."

"I'm Lucille. Lucille DeLoach."

"Lucille, can I ask you for a favor?"

"You can as' me for anything you want, Senator."

"An aide of mine is in town to help me out. Would it be okay if he came down to the party?"

"Of *course*! Tell me what hotel he's stayin' in an' I'll call him myself."

Fifteen minutes later Bill Rode was at Reuben's side, mint julep in hand. It was past seven-thirty and Reuben was finding the juleps powerful. "Powerful like a powerful bull," he told Bill. "But powerful matadors *like* powerful bulls—they like the challenge."

"You're liking the challenge of this julep, boss?"

"I'm likin'—see how I can adjust to local idiom, Bill?—I'm likin' all kinds of challenges tonight."

But he did not like the very immediate challenge he suddenly faced. A heavyset man, julep in hand, tie loosened, jaw thrust menacingly forward, stood squarely in front of Reuben. The sweat beaded on his flushed forehead as he unclenched his jaw to shout. "Heah me, y'all. Heah me. *Heah me!*"

Reuben turned his head to Lucille. "Who's this?"

"Tha's Bartle. Bartle O'Dwyer. Noisy genelman."

The tent had now gone relatively quiet, and Bartle O'Dwyer pointed a finger at Reuben. "Ladies and genelmen, this is the guy—the creepy guy—I went to in Saigon during a Vietcong raid. The gooks had got raht into the embassy grounds and we needed defensive fire. I ast for volunteers. There were six men in the office there. *Five* of them volunteered. *Not this guy*. He wanted to stay where he was, the colonel's toy lieutenant." O'Dwyer dropped his glass on the floor and brought his right fist up in a roundhouse punch aimed at Reuben's stomach. Reuben easily swerved out of the way. He thought quickly. He'd have to fight back unless—

Two guests, one of them a bulldog with huge shoulders and powerful arms, seized O'Dwyer and dragged him away, toward the bar.

The silence was momentary. In ten seconds everyone was talking again. Reuben's face was white. "Get me another—" but Lucille was already there with the fresh julep. Reuben took it, but found he had no appetite for it, or even for Lucille.

He turned to Bill Rode. "Let's go. Maybe get something to eat."

Rode accompanied him out. Several of the partygoers looked at him inquisitively—then past him.

Rode extended the iced-tea pitcher but Castle didn't extend his glass, as he had twice done after they had got back to the suite. "No more. Might interfere with my performance later on."

Rode winked an eye. "You going out on the links to practice your stroke, Senator?"

"I'm thinking of exactly that, Rode—going somewhere to practice my stroke. Rode?"

"Yes, sir?"

"What time did—what's her name? Gladys?—"

"Gladys, yes."

"—tell you she'd get here?"

"Couldn't make it before eight-thirty, she said."

"You know," Reuben's mind was wandering as, thinking better of it, he extended his glass, "I was thinking of Lucille. But not after that scene at the party."

"I'm sure Gladys will like your company, Senator."

"Why not? Most women do. All women do." He stopped and

chuckled. "I say all women. Is there any woman I haven't pleased?"

"No one who has complained to me."

"I'm not sure they'd complain to you, and they certainly would not—the nice ladies you come up with—complain to Miss America. Who else would they complain to? The secretary of commerce?"

"You don't hand out...weights and measures."

"No. But I give them a hell of a measure of what I've got to offer. If they get all I've got, they don't want anything more they can't take anything more."

The phone rang. Rode picked it up. "Yes, this is Bill Rode, Gladys. I was just leaving; I've been up here with the senator having some iced tea. Hang on." He cupped the receiver. "Should I ask her to come up?"

"No—bring her up yourself. Meet her in the lobby."

Rode spoke into the phone. "He's real anxious to say hello, Gladys. I'll be right down. Should he order dinner?" Rode smiled. "I'll tell him, Gladys. Just a little something. Bye-bye, Gladys." He leaned over to put down the phone.

CHAPTER 17

Washington, D.C., April 1987

Susan Oakeshott went early to the office on Monday to meet with her boss. She had heard about the fracas in Augusta. "It's as I hoped," she told him. "There was only a single notice about the brawler, O'Dwyer. And nothing was reported about what he said before he lunged at you."

"I take it Bill gave you the whole story?"

"Yes. And I told him not to say anything about it to anybody. Just a...a drunken guy going wild. You got out of his way and he was restrained. The only thing the people who were at that bar will be thinking about is that Hank Wright lost. Nobody's likely to hold you responsible for that."

Reuben nodded. He was in fact deeply relieved. What he had done that day in Saigon was not his favorite memory. "So then let's talk about Harold Kaltenbach."

"Yes. I've called a few people who are very reliable. Briefly, each time around, Kaltenbach bets everything he's got on one candidate for president. What he's got that counts is a network of amateurs who turn to him every four years to signal a winner. They trust his leadership, and they like the feel of a coordinated effort."

"What does Kaltenbach do—I mean, specifically?"

"He puts his candidate in touch with key players, beginning in New Hampshire—always beginning in New Hampshire, never mind what they say: Iowa comes second. He sets up meetings like three, four years ahead. He gets the pols in New Hampshire, and in Iowa and South Carolina, to organize events centered on the candidate. He pays their travel expenses, so they can come to Washington and see their candidate in action. He gets two retired congressmen—I know them both—to begin, like maybe in May, June the year before the election—in this case, it would be May or June 1991—to nourish the apparatus."

"Does he pay money?"

"Kaltenbach is the most careful, discreet man on the public scene, and he succeeds in hardly ever getting mentioned. He works through other people. But on money he's super-careful. The money that's spent comes in from volunteer organizations of the candidate's fans."

An aide brought them coffee. "How did he pass the word to you that I had . . . survived our first meeting?"

"He called me himself, the way he's been doing."

"What exactly did he say?"

"He said, 'Susan, I had a nice meeting with your boss. He may have a political future. I'd like to see him again, make sure there isn't anything that would, well, get in the way.' "

"That's when he suggested meeting on the boat?"

"Yes. He said that he doesn't like 'furtive encounters'—his words. But that nothing is served by provoking people's curiosity. He said, 'I just need a couple of hours, and no one's going to interrupt us on the *Circe*.' "

"Susan, is there anything I need to think about? I mean, that I haven't already thought about?"

"He's sure to ask you, and I mean blow by blow, what you did in Vietnam."

"And what I didn't do?"

"And what you didn't do."

"Is he likely to ask about Priscilla?"

"He will *certainly* ask about Priscilla. And if I was him, *I'd* ask about Priscilla."

"Anything more, Susan?"

"The Supreme Court's ruling is due in *United States* v. *Paradise*, the civil-rights case about the one-for-one promotion requirement in the Alabama Department of Public Safety—you promote one white, you gotta promote one black, otherwise you're discriminating. We have to keep an eye on that.

"And you should expect a call or two from candidates aiming at the 1988 primaries. I say that because I know that Governor Dukakis has already called a couple of senators."

"What did they say? I mean, the senators he called?"

"*You* know, Reuben. It's pretty easy this early on. The line is that you will work hard for the election of...the Democratic nominee. Whoever he is."

"And Harold Kaltenbach is certain that the winner this time around is going to lose to George Bush?"

"Absolutely *certain*. He didn't give any details." Susan Oakeshott stood up. "You'd better be on your way. Tell the taxi driver to take you to the Gangplank Marina on the river, just east of the Fourteenth Street Bridge. When you get there, if anybody asks, say you're going to meet somebody on the yacht *Circe*, which is on Pier 5. Leave your coat and tie here and take the jacket you wear to baseball games."

Reuben Castle, at mid-morning, gave every appearance of being a carefree, boat-bound thirty-eight-year-old. He was informally dressed, with a copy of *Time* magazine in his hand and a paperback book sticking an inch or so out of a jacket pocket. If on the pier he had bumped into the senior senator from North Dakota, no less, he'd have said, "Hello, Mark. I'm taking a few hours off today. How you doing?" ... Reuben could handle just about anything, anybody.

There was no one on duty in the marina office, so he made his way to Pier 5 and from there to *Circe*.

Kaltenbach greeted him from the stern, beckoning him up the gangway.

"Nice to see you, Senator. Let's go below. The cabin is air-conditioned and it's already getting hot out."

Reuben sat down comfortably on a sofa across from Kaltenbach. The light below was dim, and Reuben's eyes took a moment to adjust. *Circe* was an eighty-foot ketch with an unusual design belowdecks. The dining table, where Reuben now faced his inquisitor, was pierced through the center by a large painted column—the mast. Reuben shifted so that his view across the table was unimpeded. To his right, he noticed four bottles of dark rum, one of light rum, and a single glass. The channel water lapped against the hull. All around, wood creaked slowly against metal.

• • •

Kaltenbach wanted to talk about Vietnam. Had Reuben done anything to avoid serving, or to postpone serving?

Where had he trained for the army?

Had he taken any specialized courses at Fort Gordon?

Was he attached to an infantry unit?

At what point in basic training had he applied for Officer Candidate School?

On receiving his commission, had he been sent immediately to Vietnam?

Did he rejoin his unit, after being commissioned?

When he arrived in Saigon, was he still part of an army combat unit?

Who was responsible for detaching him from that unit?

When he was attached to headquarters, who was his boss?

How long did he work in headquarters?

Was it routine to stay on for a period in headquarters, once you were attached there?

The colonel's clerical staff consisted of six men. How many of them went on to combat duty?

How do you explain that you were the only lieutenant at headquarters who didn't go on to combat?

"Ask the colonel," you say? No way to do that. Okay. We move on.

Why didn't you complete law school?

What were your grades in law school?

Do you have a record of your grades?

You'll try to find those for me? Okay.

Do you have copies of faculty reports on your work? . . . You mislaid them?

Did you fail any course in law school?

So—you were drawn to public service, and then you just wanted to get on with life, make a living, start a family. Beginning in college, did you have any romances?

No. I mean anything anybody would be interested, in 1992, to hear about.

That's a nice answer, Senator. You wouldn't want the ten girlfriends you had in college to think nobody would be interested in hearing about them. Okay.

Now Mrs. Castle—Priscilla. One child, a boy, Reuben Jr. Is Mrs. Castle alone a lot?

Does she go out with other men?

Has she had any affairs?

You *assume* not? If somebody set out to prove that she did have . . . outside interests, would they find evidence?

Come on. You know what I mean. Have there been any items, gossip columns, rumors that got to you, about Priscilla?

Does she want you to become president?

Is she willing to put aside her own interests to help you in your career?

What is your financial worth?

"A couple of hundred thousand"? Plus real estate?

And Priscilla's?

You say, "Twice that." On account of Miss America?

"And an inheritance," you say. So together, for both of you, it's about a million dollars or around that?

Thanks very much, Senator. One day maybe you'll be sailing up and down the Potomac. Maybe quite a few times. Say hello to your Miss Susan.

CHAPTER 18

Boulder, December 1987

"Mom! What have you done to yourself? Is that the way you looked when you married my dad?"

"Well, darling, that was eighteen years ago. Obviously I've changed in some ways."

"But how come you can make yourself look, well, the way you must have looked back then?"

She didn't try to disguise her pleasure. Justin left the room to get a Coke, and Henrietta turned her head to look into the hallway mirror. It had been a full minute since she had last looked at herself, in the bathroom mirror. Her hair was curled over her forehead, coming down around her ears, glistening behind her long young neck. On her shoulders she wore the yellow tulle her father had given her when Justin was born, and around her neck she wore her mother's pearls. The lipstick, pink and moist, she had had to go out to buy, at Jacki Goodman's. She hadn't used lipstick for all those years.

She wondered, did she look too much like a vamp on the prowl? What would they have thought of her at the university in Paris, got up that way, in the light of her reputation for resolute drabness? Her father had once upbraided her for her neglected appearance, but her aunt Josephine, who was naturally

WILLIAM F. BUCKLEY JR.

austere, defended her. "It is perfectly right," she had told her brother, "that Henrietta should continue in mourning for her husband."

Amy had been forthright in her invitation to come for drinks and dinner. "I'm not telling you," she said over the phone, "that you have to tart yourself up. I *am* telling you that it wouldn't make any sense to arrive with your natural attractions in disguise, the way they've been since you came to Boulder. Jean-Paul may not notice if you dress up, but he would certainly notice if you came in looking like a nun."

"Jean-Paul? Have I met him?"

"Probably not, unless you've attended meetings of the French faculty. I've never encountered him in the stacks, where you and I hang out."

"Why did you invite him?"

"Because he's attractive. And a widower."

"When did his wife die?"

"You remember the Air India flight that went down?"

"Oh mon Dieu, yes! —I won't tell any jokes about airplanes."

"You are coming to life, dear Henrietta."

Also invited were Halston Rauschig and his wife, Helen. Halston was the soul of the Democratic Party in Boulder. He was pleased when Amy, in introducing him to Henrietta, took pains to point out that it had been Halston who had put together the Democratic rally the previous semester, "where Reuben Castle wowed everybody."

"Were you there?" Halston asked Henrietta.

"Yes, I was."

"What was your impression?"

"Impression of what?"

"Well, of the speaker. Senator Castle."

They were standing in the glassed-in garden room, which looked out over the mountains, still faintly visible against the early December dusk. Amy suddenly remembered: "Hey, Henri! Weren't you at the University of North Dakota, before going to Paris? Castle was also at the University of North Dakota! Did your paths cross?"

"I don't remember."

The doorbell rang and Amy went to answer it as Halston broke in: "Reuben Castle was a big shot on campus—chairman of the Student Council and editor of the student newspaper. If you were there at the same time, he'd have been hard to miss."

"My mind was on other things. I had some extracurricular activities of my own."

"Like what?" Amy Parrish asked, returning with Jean-Paul Lafayette.

"Like duck hunting."

Jean-Paul was extending his hand. "Enchanté," he said.

Henri murmured a reply, and Amy told her how lovely she looked. Helen agreed. "You're hardly dressed to go duck hunting, Henri."

"I don't know, Helen. Maybe I am."

She sat down next to Jean-Paul. His thick dark hair was cut short and curled close to his head. His gentle eyes and wry smile caught her, and his voice was light but warm. His native French was flawless, of course, but also colorful, and he insisted on using it. That was perfectly agreeable to Henri, less so to the other guests, but they all enjoyed themselves, talked politics for a bit, and ate and drank with relish, keeping John Parrish busy tending bar and pouring wine. He did manage to say to the Rauschigs—first to Halston, then separately to Helen—that the new line of Buicks, which his dealership was currently displaying, could be outfitted with a collapsible bar, "if you want one."

Halston said that if he was getting a new car he might well want one. "It would be handy to have for celebrating the Democratic victory next November!"

John poured Halston's glass full.

CHAPTER 19

Boulder, December 1987

Jean-Paul Lafayette called Henrietta's number the next morning, speaking French as usual. It was Justin who answered the phone. He was taken aback for a moment at being addressed in his native tongue. Finally: "Vous voulez parler avec Madame Durban?"

Jean-Paul answered gratefully, "Justement."

Justin bounded into the kitchen. "Mom, some frog wants you on the phone."

"Justin! Do...not...use...that...word."

"Okay." He sat down at the breakfast table, pulled up his glasses, and began to read the sports page.

It has to be Jean-Paul, Henri said to herself, walking to the phone.

He greeted her.

He had much enjoyed the dinner...."Amy is a darling....I have been talked into test-driving a Buick car. Do you know anything about Buicks, apart from what you've heard from John?"

They rattled on in French for a few enjoyable minutes.

Was Henri free to have lunch with him that day? "I am lecturing at two. Perhaps the Faculty Club at twelve-thirty?"

She questioned herself rapidly. She had never even been inside the Faculty Club. "Um, yes. That would be very nice. I would attend the lecture except that I have to be back at the library."

"I will give you the lecture at your convenience. And that way I can deliver it in French!"

The telephone rang again within minutes. It was Amy. Henri could picture her, petite and tidy, with the broad smile that reconfigured her whole face.

"Darling, you were a big hit last night. With everybody, but especially JP. 'Jean-Paul' sounds so formal. Sounds like a French opera."

"He doesn't object to 'JP'?"

"Oh, no. By the end of dinner, he was telling Halston and Helen to call him Zhay Pee."

"Listen, Amy, he called me just now. Wants me to have lunch with him at the Faculty Club."

"That's my Henrietta! You can ask him to call you Henri."

"I like him. He told me he's lecturing on Daumier this afternoon. I won't be there, but I like the way he sort of half treats me as a French student, half as a lover."

"Well, what do you know! You'll have to travel to France some day and reacquaint yourself with how those—"

"*Don't say 'those frogs.'*"

Amy laughed. "I wasn't going to. Never would use the word, let alone when talking to someone whose father was French. No, I like him too, and Professor Gauthier, the head of the French department, I know likes him. Gauthier struggled hard to persuade him to stay at the university last year."

"He wanted to quit?"

"When Stephanie died, that left him pretty wasted. He just wanted to do something else. But I think he's over that. I'm so *pleased* you've taken a shine to each other."

"Amy, I have to go. Justin's finished his breakfast and I need to take him to school. I'll report for duty at the library by nine."

"I'll be a half hour late. John insists I go by his dealership and see the new Buicks."

"You can drink from the bar in the backseat."

"Oh. You heard his line last night   "

"Got to go. See you later."

How would she dress? She'd be going to the Faculty Club right from the library. She had to act quickly. Justin mustn't be late. Anything other than her work slacks and blouse! If she wore the silk shantung skirt she'd bought last Christmas, would that be a little flashy as office wear? The hell with it. She found it deep in the closet and put it on. She put her pearls in her pocket; she'd keep them there until she left for the Faculty Club.

CHAPTER 20

Boulder, December 1987

It was Christmas Eve. Justin would leave the apartment at five o'clock to spend a happy few hours with three friends, Sarah and Paul Robbins (twins), and Hector Block. They would go to the Roxy Theater and catch the double feature. Three solid hours of moviegoing. Then Alice Robbins, the twins' mother, would pick them up, and they would have Christmas Eve supper at the Robbinses' house. At twenty minutes to twelve, Henrietta would drive over and take Justin to the midnight Mass at Saint Martin de Porres.

Meanwhile, Jean-Paul would come for her at six, and they would go for dinner at the country club.

It had been a diligent courtship. Since meeting at Amy's they had lunched or dined together a half dozen times, though never with Justin present. JP was pressing Henri hard, and she sensed that she would have to make a strategic decision tonight. She sensed it and so did he, and when he emerged from his car, in a perfectly tailored herringbone overcoat, she watched him from the window. She thought she could discern a special bounce in his step, but maybe it was the bounce in her own spirits that she was feeling.

She had chilled champagne for him.

"Show me a picture of Justin," he said.

That was easy for Henri to do. She pulled over an album. JP could examine Justin at age three, playing in the Parc Monceau; at age six, entering the Ecole Belles Feuilles; and so on. There were random snapshots with his grandfather and Nadine at the apartment on Avenue Foch, and one with Nadine setting out a cake for his twelfth birthday. The photo at the airport when they were leaving for Colorado was marked in a childish hand, "Juin, 1985. On part pour l'Amérique."

"He is a very handsome boy."

"He is my love."

"I too am your love. Isn't that so?"

She took his hand, pressed it, and refilled his glass. "I'll relieve you of Justin," she said, withdrawing the album.

"Henri, Justin is away until you pick him up for the service. May I take you to bed? Express the love I feel for you?"

Henri drew breath. She looked down at her champagne glass. "Well," she said. "Yes, JP, if you...want."

"I must, Henri, I must."

She got up and pointed to the room on her left. "That's Justin's room. You can undress there. I'll wait for you in my room." She signaled to the right.

In Boulder in December it is dark outside at six-thirty. It had been dark in the duck blind too that night, but there had been the little candle that showed her the whole of Reuben as he slid into the bedroll beside her.

She went to her dressing table, loosened two of the bulbs,

left the third one lighted, and started to disrobe. Still too much light. She dimmed the little bulb by draping her slip over it.

Then she opened her bedroom door and left it open. Through the opening she called out, "Viens, Jean-Paul."

She covered herself with a single bedsheet, and closed her eyes. He made his way onto the bed, and told her how beautiful she was, and how happy she was making him. "I will try all my life to make you happy, like me."

"You sound like Daumier."

That brought a salvific laugh, and a deep and earnest kiss.

CHAPTER 21

Boulder, December 1987

At the country club there was much festivity, including three live Santa Clauses. The first two hours were given over to pleasing the children. At approximately eight-thirty the kids left, and the adults were seated in the dining room. Used as a ballroom in the club's richer days, the large hall had now been partitioned into two smaller spaces. Jean-Paul and Henri's table was far from the incongruous wall, which stood out bare and obvious alongside the crown moldings and rich baseboards of the others. Electric sconces dotted the papered walls, and the floor, once polished crisp wood for dancing, was now carpeted. Two dozen round tables were arranged in what remained of the grand old room; they were draped in white—spare, but elegantly set. The club was no richer than its patrons, who, mostly hailing from the university, were pleased simply to have someplace to relax in a little style.

Henri wondered whether she herself looked as starry-eyed as Jean-Paul did. She enjoyed probing her memory on the act of love, in which she had just now, with surprising pleasure, engaged. She had read that men, mostly younger men to be sure, exchanged information—when meeting in locker rooms or clubs or around the bar—on whom they had bedded, and how. She thought such conversations vulgar and certainly intrusive.... But what kind of thing might be said in these exchanges interested her. She was, simply, curious.

Reuben had told her at the duck blind that he had never "done it" before. She trusted him to be telling her the truth, although, lacking any experience by which to judge, she could not be entirely sure at the time whether his conduct that night gainsaid what he had told her. All that had distilled in her memory was that the very first time, in September 1969, his handling of himself—and of her—was clumsy by comparison with the finesse of their final copulation four months later.

This had taken place at the motel in Minneapolis. He had driven her there, on the first leg of her long voyage to Paris, in order to "do it one last time." After the baby was born, after Reuben had graduated from UND, they would be reunited and would do it—every night! She had hoped so, most fervently; and tonight, after an eighteen-year hiatus, she allowed herself to think about the differences in technique between Reuben, the twenty-one-year-old undergraduate, and Jean-Paul, the widower Frenchman of polish and God knows how much experience gained during his youth in France, and then during his marriage to Stephanie.

He knew, certainly, how to engage her physically, how to bring on the transformation. But was she—Henri—an important component of his elation? A critical component of it? Or could a doxy, French or American, have done as much for him? To him? She resolved to assume that she was—herself—in some way unique. Looking over at him now as he looked down at the menu, she found it easy to think of *him* as unique.

He did not mention their lovemaking; nor did she expect that he would. But after the dessert and brandy, and with only a half hour left before she would set out to pick up Justin, he said he wanted to talk with her about plans for the future.

"At some point, of course, when we're married, you will move in with me, or I'll move in with you. Between now and then we will need to make suitable arrangements." He was glad that the conversation, in French, permitted him to speak of "affaires de convenance," which was easier to handle than "matters of convenience." "I'll cooperate in any way you wish, but I do think that early in the new year we should give out the happy news that we intend to be married."

She put down her coffee. "Darling JP. I cannot marry you."

He was stupefied. He fumbled for the right words and finally said, merely, "Why?"

"Because I am already married."

He couldn't make that out. He said, "Your husband was killed in Vietnam."

"That's the story I give out. That's the story I've always told Justin."

"In fact—he wasn't killed? He left you?"

"Yes."

"How is that possible?"

She paused. "We're not going to discuss that aspect of it, surely—why he left me."

"I assume he has remarried? Surely that dissolves your marriage."

"Actually, no. If one partner commits bigamy, the marriage is not annulled."

"I decline to take this matter seriously. You are talking, dear Henri, about a marriage that has not been active for—what?—eighteen years?"

"Yes."

"A civil marriage? That should make things relatively easy."

"Our marriage was, I assume, both civil and religious. —Speaking of which, JP, I must pick up my son and take him to church." She stood up. "I'm not going to kiss you, Jean-Paul, in a public room. Know that I love you truly. I will pray tonight for guidance."

He led her out the door to where she had parked her car.

CHAPTER 22

Harrison Ledyard had foreseen, from very early days, that his friendship with Jean-Paul would turn out to be time-consuming. The friendship was nurtured when the two young men, whose wives were first cousins, lived in Washington, both studying at Georgetown, Jean-Paul at the graduate school, Harrison at the law school. Jean-Paul was, after all, a Frenchman. Frenchmen are always troublesome, Ledyard thought resignedly. And Jean-Paul's being a Frenchman living and working in America naturally augmented the problems.

But the friendship between the two young couples had been strong, and heartily endorsed by all four parties to it: Harrison and Melissa Ledyard, and Jean-Paul and Stephanie Lafayette. For one thing, Harrison was temperamentally that kind of friend, the kind that works at friendship. For another, JP and Stephanie, when they were living in France, had shown the Ledyards the ultimate kindness: they took into their home the Ledyard daughter, Teresa. They gave her a room in their house in Neuilly when, at age sixteen, she said she would like to do a year's schooling in Paris and would most happily do this in the company of the Lafayettes, the couple she had known so well in Washington.

Ledyard had stayed on at Georgetown, moving on quickly

from student of law to professor of law and affiliate of the blue-chip firm of Covington & Burling, for which he did estate work. He was familiar with JP's finances because the two cousins' grandmother had died shortly before the plane crash that took Stephanie's life. Harrison had handled the grandmother's estate on behalf of the two parties, the live granddaughter and the estate of the dead granddaughter.

Ledyard knew his friend JP to be a thorough and ambitious scholar, conscientiously committed to doing his best at whatever job he had in hand. As of January 1988, this job was to serve as professor of French literature at the University of Colorado. The death of Stephanie had meant an influx of funds for the benefit of Jean-Paul, since theirs had been a childless marriage. This lessened the need for JP to concern himself with earning a living. He was financially independent enough to be able to tailor his obligations to the University of Colorado in whatever way was satisfactory to both parties. What he wasn't free to do, however, was marry his new lady, Henrietta Durban.

"Harrison, surely there is something in the law that rescinds a marriage not...exercised? I mean, we are talking about a marriage contracted, I take it, in 1969—perhaps early 1970—with no subsequent interaction between bride and groom."

"No. There is no such provision as you're reaching for in the law. In theology, a marriage is annullable if never consummated. Your lady—"

"Henrietta."

"Henrietta has the son—Justin—so that would not apply to her, the hypothesis that the marriage was never consummated. And there is the further complication: civil law doesn't always harmonize with religious law. She—Henrietta—is a practicing Catholic?"

"Oh, very much so. She takes, well, liberties with the Ten Commandments, but she is structurally a member of the Church. For that matter, so am I."

"I knew that, JP. Just trying to tie the strands together. As you tell it, neither of the married parties has sought a divorce. That's right, isn't it?"

"I assume Henri would have told me if she herself had ever sued for divorce. If her husband took the initiative, whatever ensued would be part of a court record, right?"

"Goddam it, JP, find out where in hell the marriage took place. We've got to get details of that kind, otherwise we're helpless."

"But JP, I don't *want* to go into it." As ever, they were talking in French. "You want me to stir up a hornet's nest. It would be painful to do this. And if I succeeded in getting a civil divorce, what would that do about the marriage in the eyes of God? What reason is there to conclude that the marriage— the *marriage*, JP—can be annulled? Can an annulment take place if the petition for annulment is not endorsed by both parties?"

"Of course it can, Henri. Recall the wedding of George IV to Caroline. His marriage to Mrs. Fitzherbert was annulled, and God knows she made a fuss about that, banging on the doors of Westminster Abbey!"

"JP, cher Jean-Paul, I do not want such an exercise. I don't want to protest anything."

WILLIAM F. BUCKLEY JR.

"Then you do not want to marry me."

"You have to understand what I am saying. I *am married*. My husband is unfaithful. And I have been unfaithful. But I have to be faithful to the eternal vows I made."

Jean-Paul rose from the sofa. "I have to think things through."

"Yes. And so must I—my beloved Jean-Paul," she said. "But call me when you feel like it. And"—she did not try to contain the tears—"take me in your arms, whenever you want."

CHAPTER 23

Boulder, April 1988

Justin approached Amy in the spring. He was nearly eighteen, he reminded himself, and not inexperienced in the vicissitudes of life. He had learned early that life could be sharp and arbitrary. There had been the shock of his grandfather's death when he was fourteen; then the loss of his great-aunt to the convent; then the wrenching separation from his nurse-protector, Nadine, as he and his mother made the trip into another world, one he had only read about. Of course, he knew English, which his mother had taught him from infancy. But now he had to speak in English day and night. He had had to make a fresh set of friends, and there were new demands at school—it had never occurred to him that the United States had a history, let alone one he would be expected to master. He had learned what every boy learns at puberty, and then there was the special situation at home, he and his mother, with no father.

He thought himself entirely adult in important matters, notably in his concern for his mother, which had evolved into a sense of responsibility for her. But with it all he was still a very young observer of the world around him, with a lanky, obstinate concern to know life and its mysteries.

• • •

The whole sexual scene had descended on him the previous spring. There were the hints and allusions that Paul would make about various teachers, and now even about Sarah—Paul's twin sister! She had been an integral member of their team; no longer. Now it was Justin and Paul. Paul brought to their rendezvous the scintillating erotic books, some of them even illustrated. Then came the night at the campsite with Paul, in the pup tent. All alone, except for the battery-powered portable television—and the movie. *Deep Throat.* Justin felt a stirring in his loins not felt keenly before, but now suddenly demanding. He said to Paul in quite solemn tones, "You know what, Paul? We need to get laid."

Paul agreed, though he was apprehensive about it.

They would do it in Denver, during the summer vacation. Justin would cautiously, but diligently, inquire about just where to go to do it—to have it done—how much it would cost, whether tips were appropriate, all those things. He was a quick learner and in weeks knew everything that was within the reach of an energetic sixteen-year-old living in a sophisticated academic community and bent on exploring that great key to social behavior, social relations, social protocols, and human passions.

All of that—and then Mr. Lafayette entering his life. He thought it urbane, on meeting him, to call him "Général Lafayette," as though this Lafayette were the great marquis. Jean-Paul thought this amusing and invited Justin to continue calling him "*mon général.*"

And then, for the first time Justin could remember, his mother started going out in the evening. Sometimes she would call him, or manage to get a note to him, saying she would be working late and going out to dine with colleagues. But several times she had exactly ascertained when Justin would be leaving the apartment, as he often did to watch a sports event with a friend, or to join someone in a study session before an exam. One evening he waited across the street, his bicycle parked around the corner, and saw Général Lafayette approach the entrance to the building. Justin did not stay there on watch, waiting for his mother's guest to depart, but he permitted himself to wonder whether, when he was away on other evenings, and on occasional weekends, Général Lafayette was keeping his mother company.

Justin went to Amy a few weeks later. He trusted her. And he knew that his mother trusted her. From Amy he wanted to know more about his mother, beginning with her background.

Amy told him only that Henrietta did not talk about her married days, "before you were even born, Justin." Amy felt that Henrietta's privacy should be respected, and that Justin should feel the same way about it. "You're a darling boy and your mother loves you, so don't make life difficult for her."

Justin had no intention in the world of respecting his mother's privacy.

He had for some time contemplated probing the locker in her closet. He knew only that it existed. But the idea of getting to know more than that had germinated, and he waited impatiently for a convenient time. One Thursday his mother spoke of a late afternoon staff meeting at the Chinook Library.

He got back from school and went to her bedroom. Her closet had no lock. In a corner, behind where her clothes hung, he found a bookcase and in it a leather case about the size of a shoe box.

He lifted it to her bed. It was locked with a simple combination lock. It was a matter of minutes before he had contrived to open it. He had tried first his mother's birthday—9-8-4-8—which failed. Then his own—5-6-7-0—which worked. He opened the case and found his mother's birth certificate, his own birth certificate ("Justin Raymond Durban"), her passport, his own passport, 20,000 French francs in 100-franc bills, and a Crédit Lyonnais bank book. There had been no transactions in the three years since they left France, and the book showed a total of 150,000 francs. He whistled. That would translate to about $25,000. Her patrimony, he surmised.

There were letters, perhaps a dozen. He did not have the heart to inspect these, but he looked with special interest at a photograph, in a slender wooden frame, of a young man, perhaps nineteen or twenty years old. It bore only the notation, in ink, "September, 1969." The young man was smiling—or was he laughing? His hair was loose in the breeze, his hand gripping a jacket of some sort, a parka perhaps. He was conspicuously American, pleasing to look at, carefree, manifestly at home in the outdoors. This—Justin felt the sweat on his brow—must be his father. And it was the same man he had seen and heard at the Democratic rally the year before. He was looking at a photograph of Reuben Castle.

Justin scooted to his own room for his camera. He photographed his birth certificate, his mother's passport, and then the photograph.

He put everything carefully back in place, and carried away this secret knowledge in silence.

One day, he promised himself, he would uncover the whole story.

BOOK THREE

CHAPTER 24

Honolulu, Hawaii, February 1972

When he walked down the gangplank of the SS *Helmsley* in Honolulu, Lieutenant Reuben Castle was off his stride. He left behind on the navy transport vessel 1,082 men, going home after fighting a losing war. Their destination—the next stop after twelve hours of reprovisioning—was San Luis Obispo, California, where rapid discharge papers would be made out. The restless, bored soldiers were not permitted shore leave in Hawaii, even for a few modest hours.

Castle was happy to leave the ship, but a little apprehensive about being alone for the first time in a year and a half. Two days before, Lieutenant Castle had been handed a dispatch by a courier from the radio room. It was from the Department of Defense. The first line caught his eye. His father was dead.

He knew what the letter would go on to say. As a duty officer at the Personnel Deployment Office with the Fourth Infantry Division in Vietnam, he was familiar with bureaucratic army prose. He had seen dozens of dispatches notifying soldiers of deaths in their families, and it had been his job to relay to the Pentagon word of soldiers lost in action. These dispatches in turn generated letters carrying the bad news and extending the condolences of the nation, signed by the president.

Late one night, after much drink with Bill Sulla, Reuben thought of devising different form letters for the army to use. This permitted a little morbid fun, but the two young men didn't act on the idea. "Look, Reuben," Bill said the next day, "these notices have to be utilitarian. You can bring out the violins when it's a soldier who has been killed, but you can't get in anything weepy if it's a dead parent. How can you expect the Department of Defense to know if you and Dad even got along?"

First Lieutenant William Sulla, West Point Class of 1970, was a practical man, except for what Reuben considered his insane desire to court death. After a mere three months serving at Personnel, where the job was to route incoming soldiers to their destinations, Sulla began his agitation to be assigned to combat duty. "What's your hurry?" Reuben asked him. But he didn't pursue the point. Bill Sulla, West Pointer, had accepted that fighting the war was the main task in South Vietnam. And that was what he wanted to do.

Sulla got his way after just three months of petitioning. In early May, the tall, bronzed lieutenant—he managed one hour per day of South Vietnam sun during his desk duty—was formally assigned to the First Battalion, Eighth Infantry. But exactly six weeks later he was back at his old desk at headquarters, assigning other American soldiers to combat. Bill Sulla had led his infantry platoon on a mission and on day two set off a land mine, happily underpowered. He suffered a leg wound. The Purple Heart injury was not incapacitating, but under the get-'em-home regulations in force by that point in the war, Lieutenant Sulla was told he was entitled to return to the United States. He didn't want to leave, though. Not until he was ordered to leave. He felt he owed West Point active duty for two years.

"Okay, Lieutenant." Sulla was being spoken to by Major O'Reilly, personnel officer. O'Reilly was a bearded veteran, by nature ruler of the roost. He'd have been efficient—and content—managing a truck depot. "We'll let you stand in at the personnel desk. I suppose I could say that if Colonel Sapperly" (the staff called him "Colonel Sarsaparilla") "was on duty today he'd have called out a parade to honor your sacrifice."

"Cut it out, Major."

"Okay, okay. Anyway, nice show. Go back and report in to Lieutenant Castle. You're familiar with responsibilities there." So Bill Sulla returned to the PDO, working next to Reuben Castle, who never left the office during the day, not even to catch the sun.

Reuben was handed the DOD letter as the liner trod tirelessly over placid hot seas, bearing toward Hawaii at twenty-one knots. The letter informed him of the death of his only living relative. He explained it to Bill Sulla, who had seven siblings. "My mother died soon after I was born. I have no aunts, no uncles, no siblings, no—" Reuben paused for an instant "—no offspring."

The news brought back the memory of a phone call he had received during his dwindling days at UND. Reuben had been relieved when his father told him that he did not want to attend any ceremony or celebration other than the commencement itself. "You know, Reub, I don't mix things up very well, lots of people around I don't know. Your mother was good at it and you inherited all her way of doing things. You'll go into politics one of these days, I know. Well, you're in politics now, in a way. You ever lose an election?"

"I guess I didn't ever, Dad. But I've got a new election coming up."

"What's that?"

"I'm going to apply for law school."

"When?"

"Well, right away. Usually the law schools like applications to come in six months before term starts. If they insist on that, I'll have to go for spring term to start in."

"Spring term when?"

"Well, spring term next year."

"What does your draft board tell you about that?"

"If I'm actually *in* school, I'm safe."

"Safe from what? From Vietnamese gunfire?"

"Well—well, yes, obviously. They're not going to come over and shoot me here."

"Now, look here, Reuben. I want you alive. But not as a man who refuses to do his duty. It's okay to criticize policy, and you've done that enough. But now you're soldier age and if the draft board tells you it's your turn to fight, then it's your turn to fight. When I get to your commencement I want to know what day you're signing up."

And that had been that.

The message advising Reuben of his father's death had a practical side. Details were given in a printed paragraph from the adjutant. Lieutenant Castle was entitled, under existing regulations, to request discharge from the ship's roster at "the next port of call"—in this case, Honolulu—leaving him free to

put in for a slot on an air force transport, to expedite family funeral arrangements. Such transport flights left every few hours,
carrying personnel and special equipment from Hawaii to "the
mainland"—idiomatic use in Hawaii to designate the continental United States.

Reuben had plenty of time to reflect on his options. Honolulu was thirty-two hours away.

Yes, Bill Sulla was familiar with the office in which he had
worked for six months. At the Personnel Deployment Office,
four officers, two warrant officers, and six enlisted clerks decided, weighing demands, where to send the men who arrived
from training in the States. In the months Sulla had served there
before moving on to combat duty, a half million men had been
processed, arriving in Saigon and fanning out to do duty as artil-
lerymen, snipers, cooks, and orderlies. They had come and gone
through the PDO, more than three thousand of them shipped
back in caskets.

Bill Sulla had spent many hours with Reuben Castle, but not
many discussing the war in which they were both engaged. They
talked about everything else. Bill found Reuben astonishingly
well informed on what was going on in the noncombat world.
He admired Reuben's capacity for work and his skillful alloca-
tion of his energies—Reuben Castle always had time to address
any problem, and time to engage in any diversion. He managed,
even, to feign interest in what it had been like spending four
years at West Point.

Routinely, individual officers working at the PDO were sent
out for duty in the field after a few months. It was to advance

himself on that combat-duty list that Sulla had labored. That summer and fall, back at the PDO, he allowed himself to wonder how it was that Castle's name never appeared on the combat-duty roster, even though he had been much longer than six months at headquarters. Sulla did not bring up the point, but he could not help noticing that Castle cultivated the approval of the middle-aged, shrewd-eyed soldier most directly in charge of the weekly shuffle of names which moved personnel from clerical to combat status. This clerk was a mere sergeant, though a master sergeant of over thirty years' service. Young lieutenants would come for a few months to the PDO, then go out with fighting units. Reuben Castle would always see them off, sometimes buying the beer at the good-bye affairs.

Bill Sulla declined to harbor any thought that cowardice was a factor. He liked Reuben too much to indulge any such suspicion. Reuben's permanence in Saigon was just the luck of the draw, Bill told himself.

Eventually the day came to disassemble the PDO—not enough U.S. soldiers were coming in to South Vietnam any more to justify a continuation of the personnel unit. Those who arrived could be deployed by a computer operating out of Hawaii. And so Reuben and Bill found themselves sharing with two other officers a tiny cabin on the SS *Helmsley*, bound for Honolulu. Nobody, by the beginning of 1972, was clamoring for combat duty. Not in Saigon, not at the Pentagon.

CHAPTER 25

At Sea, February 1972

Lieutenant Castle reported to the adjutant later in the afternoon that he would avail himself of the offer to expedite his travel schedule so that he could fly to his father's funeral.

By the end of the day, he had in hand a schedule and a flight authorization form. He would disembark from the *Helmsley* with the landing crew. An army car would take him to Hickam Air Force Base. The flight voucher, on presentation to the dispatch office at the airfield, would qualify him to board the next transport bound for a stateside base. From there, he would have to make his own arrangements to get to Fargo, North Dakota.

The sergeant who handed him the papers blew smoke into his large typewriter. "It's the best we can do, Lieutenant, and not bad. We'll be in Honolulu Wednesday, 1000. You should be flying by noon, make it in four, five hours to California. Or who knows; maybe there'll be a flight going to Seattle. That would make it easier for you, since your destination is North Dakota."

"That's right, Sergeant."

"Anyway, you've got a ten-day leave before you're due to report for your discharge. You might want to do that someplace closer to—"

"Fargo."

"Fargo. Maybe Rock Island? That's near Chicago. Up to you, Lieutenant."

Reuben nodded, took his papers, and joined up with Bill Sulla for chow at 1745.

Bill said he was disconcerted that the balance of the trip would be without the company of Reuben.

"We'll stay in touch, Bill."

"Yes, and we have something to celebrate—the end of our war."

It wasn't easy to secure privacy on the great ship with a thousand men aboard. But resourceful men of war always knew how to do it, and as the sun was going down, on February 10, 1972, the ship easing into the western hemisphere, Bill and Reuben were shielded from view by a longboat's protective shadow. Bill brought out the flask and the two paper cups.

"This is good stuff," Sulla said, his eyes alight. "Cognac. French. We'll drink the whole pint. Don't worry, Reuben, don't worry. I'll resupply in Honolulu. Here's to your father, Reuben."

"It's been great to . . . to be your friend, Bill."

Twenty-four hours later Castle plopped his seabag on his shoulder, made his way through the busy lobby of the air base north of the city, and paused at the bank of telephones. He thought to telephone Mrs. Walker, a family friend, who had taken the initiative in getting the word to Reuben of his father's death.

On the other hand, what would he say?

The hell with it. He had told the adjutant on the *Helmsley* that he had gotten through to Fargo on the shipboard telephone, released for emergency use, and learned that since there was a possibility Joachim Castle's son would be there, the funeral was being put back two days. In fact Reuben hadn't made the call, and he had no intention of traveling to Fargo in midwinter.

He had quickly decided, on learning that the aircraft he was placed on would land in San Francisco, to stay there, spend the week in town. Reuben was always thinking of something to do, some challenge to meet. He had met the challenge of "fighting" in Vietnam, met the challenge—he smiled inwardly—of surviving the bloodshed. Now he was in a glamorous city of the world with no scheduled obligations, other than to report for discharge in ten days at any U.S. army center. And then? And then resume his normal life, discerning a challenge, meeting it, excelling at whatever he did, and reminding destiny that he was back in town.

What now, golden boy? World conqueror! Editor in chief! Student Council chairman! North Central Chairman of Students for Peace Now!

But for now he allowed his thinking to focus on simple pleasures he had forgone, in parts of the world he had only just tasted. He had what he thought of as big money in his pockets: he hadn't sent any home while in the service, and his winnings at poker exceeded his expenses in Saigon. He would just look around a bit.

On his way to Vietnam he had spent two nights in San Francisco, so he knew to point the taxi toward the lively Mexican bar on Fresno Street. There he had spent carefree hours, waking up late in one of the rooms upstairs. Maybe Angelina was still there? He was everything he had been fifteen months ago, plus, now, a war hero. He had been irresistible in 1970; he would be

WILLIAM F. BUCKLEY JR.

all the more so in 1972. He just needed a little time to rise and shine.

Walking into the bar, his service ribbons resplendent, the silver bar on his shirt collar glistening, he managed a little smile for the short, olive-skinned Mexican who took his bag into the lobby, the door to the bar left open, letting in the bouncy notes of the welcoming music, *¡Al fin! ¡Al fin! Ya llegaste, mi amor.*

CHAPTER 26

South Bend, Indiana, February 1989

The spring term of freshman year at Notre Dame was full for Justin Durban, Class of 1992. He was enrolled in the requisite five academic courses. He was competing to join the staff of the student newspaper, *The Observer.* And for ten hours every week, he waited on tables. The system at Notre Dame was straightforward: bursary students would work for ten hours a week (in freshman year this always meant work in the dining hall) in exchange for their meals—twenty-one meals a week.

A fair enough bargain, Justin thought, but add to it the three or four hours required every day at *The Observer,* and this meant an hour or two chopped away from sleep time.

But it was exciting to Justin, and he thrived on devising stories about campus news, interviewing visiting celebrities, conspiring in fun and fancies, and learning to type without looking down at the keyboard. The accepted attitude toward the senior editors was a balance between servility and independence. Some competitors, he thought, traded openly on their affability, but Justin was naturally forthright. On one occasion he told the managing editor that he did not wish to follow a certain visiting politician around when he came to campus. "I've read up on Senator Castle in the morgue, and I heard him speak a couple of years ago in Boulder. No thanks."

It was not unheard of for a competitor to ask for a substitute assignment, and the managing editor, Mark Howard, gave the Castle story to another freshman. But at ten that night, as copy was making its way to the editors' desks, Mark looked up at Justin, who was at hand with the story he had taken on. "What's this about Senator Castle? He's a very hot number on the political scene. You got a personal problem there?"

"Yes," Justin said. "At least I think so."

Mark said nothing more. He took Justin's story and put it on the pile of copy he had to read, correct, and send down to the printer before the one A.M. deadline. "Okay, Justin. Just curious."

Late in the afternoon on election day at *The Observer*, the student candidates were lined up in the production room. Justin's election as an assistant editor was announced, along with that of ten other competitors, six of them girls. Their rankings were made public on the bulletin board, and Justin had come in first. "That means," said Janet Rudo, who ranked second, "that you'd have to buy the beer tonight. If we could get beer. And if we were allowed to drink it."

Although he prided himself on his skills as a reporter, Justin would not have been able to report what exactly had happened in the three hours after dinner. What emphatically happened after that was that he woke at six with a hangover, and the breakfast platters of sausages he had to serve out in the dining hall made him swear that he would never again willingly look at a sausage. But at eight-fifty, just before the hour on classical civilization with Professor Pfansteil, he made it to a public telephone and rang his mother's number, collect.

She said she was very very proud of him.

CHAPTER 27

Urbana, Illinois, February 1973

Reuben attended class at law school irregularly. As always, he
was able to cope. Here, doing so required a combination of tac-
tical reading before the exams, carefully tuned collaboration
with fellow students when papers were due, and a certain reli-
ance on his continuing power to make friends. There was the
exception of the starchy dean, who called him in twice to complain about his poor class attendance. "You have a place in our
law school, Mr. Castle, coveted by a great many applicants. We
gave you special consideration because you are a veteran—"

"Yes, I appreciate that, Dean. And I am very eager to do well
at the University of Illinois Law School. I will certainly pay
greater attention to class attendance—"

"Yes. I trust you will. No doubt you have heard it said that
while it is difficult to get into our law school, it is also difficult
to fail once admitted. But you are a man"—the dean looked
down at a document headed, "CASTLE, Reuben Hardwick"—
"who appears to have broken many records in the past, as a student at the University of North Dakota, and as an unharmed
officer in Vietnam."

That was the first session with Dean Blankenship. The second was more perfunctory, and more threatening.

"If you don't do better in the exams in May, you should not count on entering second-year studies in September."

Reuben nodded. Yes, sir, he understood. Yes, sir, he would do something about those late papers and poor exams.

But he didn't, and in May he was given a probationary grade. He would be entitled to register for his second year, but only after submitting to examinations to make up for work not completed in his first year. He would be entitled to take these examinations twice if necessary, on dates arranged with the dean.

There was also the problem of money. The GI Bill looked after tuition and most of the cost of room and board, but it left Reuben with nothing for casual expenses, and he did not relish living with the intrusions of financial concerns. Restless, he answered a summons from Henry Walford, chairman of the Illinois State Democratic Party. Word had gotten through to Walford, from the party head in Bismarck, North Dakota, that young Castle had been, sure, something of a hell-raiser as an undergraduate at UND—"one of those continuous rebels. But he swept the opposition away in everything he got into, and he is a fine speaker. I've invited him to speak at this year's state Democratic convention in Fargo. We're nursing our wounds since the McGovern collapse last fall, and we need a little spirit from young people. I'll let you know how it goes."

It went very well. Reuben was cautious in his references to the Vietnam War. He made certain that the state chairman knew to introduce him as a veteran of the war, with twenty months of active duty. It was not yet time, he sensed, to speak routinely of the "disastrous war," or of the "Republican war." Too many citizens of different ages had invested in the war, directly and indirectly. "There was a lot that some good people were fighting for—some South Vietnamese are still fighting for, ladies and gentlemen. The president of South Vietnam couldn't pass a political hygiene test in the state of North Dakota, but he wants something better than the South Vietnamese would get from the Vietcong."

He spoke of the need for American Democrats to press "the war against corruption in our own government" and predicted, no less, that President Nixon would be impeached.

"He got an uproarious cheer," the North Dakota Democratic leader reported to his Illinois counterpart. "That Watergate business is moving very fast, Henry."

"I'm not sure we want this young man going around at Democratic meetings in Illinois calling for the impeachment of the president," Walford replied. "But I'll get in touch with him."

It proved to be an immediately productive association. Reuben's appearance at the Democratic Labor Day rally was cheered a full four minutes before the speaker was let go. Henry Walford's desk was deluged with invitations from organizations wanting young Castle to speak. They were mostly political at first but, after a few months, not confined to Democratic Party events.

It was after the speech to the Young Presidents Club in Chicago that Reuben thought to approach his situation with strategic attention. He told Walford that he hadn't yet decided whether he was going back to law school in September 1974. Meanwhile, he would be willing to work formally with the Democratic Party organization, or informally with Walford and his law associates in Urbana and Chicago, and see what came of it.

In six months, Reuben had emerged as the voice of young

progressive America in the northern part of the state: a voice unconstricted by Republican cynicism, unburdened by responsibility for the dissolution of democracy in Vietnam, eager to foster opportunities for young Americans and "long comfortable lives for older Americans." A few weeks after opening his own office in Springfield, he traveled to Denver as a speaker for the American Federation of Television and Radio Artists. He was escorted to the head table by Priscilla Avery, a local girl who one year earlier had been crowned Miss America.

His speech, centering on the great mission of the United States in the latter part of the century, was warmly received, and when he returned to his seat at the table, Miss America gave him a kiss, which he returned ardently, bringing on cheers from many of the 300 diners.

CHAPTER 28

Boulder/South Bend, September 1989

Justin had to be ready for Gunnar, the senior at Notre Dame who had twice offered him a ride, Boulder–South Bend, in return for twenty-five dollars toward expenses and shared duty at the wheel. There had been a delay in Justin's getting his driver's license, but Henri was satisfied finally by what the ophthalmologist said: the astigmatism had leveled off. Justin would continue to need glasses to read, and could try contact lenses if he wanted to. But in any case, he had vision good enough to drive.

Gunnar was on time, at the distressing hour of nine P.M. He liked to drive all night, and Henri had not devised a means of slowing down this track star who treated twenty hours of driving, starting after dark, as simply one more 100-meter dash. She helped Justin pile his bags into Gunnar's hearty Oldsmobile, and kissed both young men good-bye.

They arrived at South Bend late on Thursday afternoon. Gunnar stopped the car outside Dillon Hall and helped Justin get his bags out of the car and onto the grass alongside. Justin would manage on his own to get them up to his room.

Back in May, *The Observer* had reported that the Student Council was protesting Notre Dame's arbitrary procedures for roommate assignments. But reforms at Notre Dame took a long time, and Justin had known nothing more, when he left South Bend in June, than that he would have a different roommate in the fall. The young man he had been sharing quarters with was quitting school. "I'll probably regret it beginning in October," Jesse Baker had said, "but I just can't turn down this offer in Silicon Valley. If I make out, I'll build a wing at Notre Dame just for you, Justin, and you won't have any more roommates to worry about."

Checking in now with the dormitory office, Justin learned that his new roommate would be someone called Allard de Minveille, the son of the Canadian ambassador to the United States. Allard was new at Notre Dame. His first year of college studies had been done at Cambridge, his father then serving in London as deputy high commissioner.

Justin would miss Jesse, but Allard, born and raised in Quebec, gave promise of being not without interest.

Justin arrived breathless at the second floor, lugging his two heavy bags. He found the spacious room he would share with Allard all but filled with bags and books and sporting equipment, including a set of golf clubs. Allard was not there, but his belongings were everywhere. Justin made his way across the room and started stuffing his own gear into the shelves on the right side of the closet. ("One of us has to get the right side; why not me?") He put books and shoes on the lower bed—let M. Allard occupy the upper bunk. After all, Justin had some seniority, having been at Notre Dame for a full year.

"Espèce de con!" Justin heard the thud and then the voice. He turned around and saw a young man, dressed in polo shirt and chinos, struggling to lift himself up from the floor. Books tucked under both arms, he had fallen over one of Justin's emptied suitcases.

His hands on the floor, he looked up. His smile made its way through the tousled hair.

Justin, also speaking in French, said, "You must be Allard. Welcome to Notre Dame. But watch your language, or they won't let you on the golf course. This is a religious school!"

Allard broke into a smile. Continuing in French he said, "I'm Allard de Minveille. Please take me to where I can get something decent to eat."

"I know a nice place. It's about a thousand miles from here."

They had dinner at McDonald's and made friends.

CHAPTER 29

Washington/Urbana, April 1990

The defeat of candidate Michael Dukakis in November 1988 had rattled the Democratic establishment, but the defeat itself wasn't entirely surprising. The party elders had hoped that the popularity of Ronald Reagan would fall finally into the abyss of unreality and confusion and resentment which, informed Americans agreed, was there, waiting to swallow up the memory of Reaganomics and the evil empire.

But in fact President Reagan and Reaganism were not run out of Washington in disgrace. He was an old man, as the wise man Walter Lippmann would have pointed out—let him just go home. Then too, Governor Dukakis was not a commanding figure and did not succeed in mobilizing the sleepy masses of the oppressed and forgotten. Finally, Vice President George H. W. Bush was a politician of striking decency, and his weltanschauung was manifestly free of Reaganite voodoo accretions. So? It would take a little while before the political restitution could be effected. *Next time out.*

By the spring of 1990 Reuben Castle could see, however indistinctly, little sparklers in his own solar system. He was hardly ready for a Secret Service detail. Yet it was an observable fact that when he traveled, when he went to colleges and assemblies to speak, his hosts felt an imperative to look after details of the engagement that reflected an unspoken sense of entitlement. Senator Castle had become a national political figure. Granted, the leadership of the Democratic Party was in the hands, if by no means securely, of a political community in which Reuben Castle, sometime youthful activist, was alien. There were plenty of reasons, in the great political derby of 1992 coming up, to skip over Senator Castle. He was young, relatively inexperienced, and the representative of a state the mention of which brought on such comments as, "Isn't that where Senator McGovern came from?" The answer to that was no—Castle was from the other Dakota, *North* Dakota. But the mere mention of the remote plains state hemmed in by Minnesota and Montana had slightly derisive overtones.

There were ever so many challenges lying ahead, but every now and then Reuben felt the guidance of his mysterious angel, Kaltenbach. Sometimes the directives were forthright. These would come to him through Susan.

"Senator"—she always addressed him so if there was anyone else within hearing—"you'll be getting a request to take part in a symposium with General Westmoreland. The University of Illinois, in October. The subject is 'Vietnam—Was It Worth It?' "

Bill Rode picked up his mail and withdrew to his own office, leaving Susan alone with Reuben in the main office.

"Harold wants to know what you think about it. He's not wild for you to do it. He said to tell you it's tough to share a platform with a general arguing on the other side, especially if the general is a national hero. But he says that if you feel you want to put something on the record about Vietnam, your consolidated view on the war, this would be a good forum."

"Sit down, Susan. Let's think together about this one. Everybody knows I was a protester."

"But everybody also knows you went on to service in Vietnam."

"Yes. And General Westmoreland isn't going to say anything about my not being assigned to combat duty in Vietnam—I was under his direct command, after all."

"The University of Illinois is also where you didn't finish law school."

"Yeah. But they—the anti-Castle types—wouldn't be looking for 1973 law-school grades, and wouldn't be able to find them if they tried. There'd be a wisecrack maybe, by the guy who introduces me, nothing more.

"No, it's the Vietnam thing. My position would be: (1) It was the wrong war. (2) The way we got into it challenges the constitutional separation of powers. (3) We can't ever forget the sacrifices or the patriotism of those who answered a call to duty.

"Sound good?"

"You have a way of making things sound good, Senator. That's why you're—why we're here."

"OK. Let's go with it."

He decided to make a full day of it, as he often did at important ports of call. He arrived in Urbana at nine o'clock the night before, and was met at the airport by the vice president of the Student Forum, Jane Sander. She drove him to his hotel and got out of the car with him. "Just thought I'd check tomorrow's schedule with you, Senator."

His day began with a seven A.M. interview on the student radio station. It was scheduled to last fifteen minutes, but at the end of the quarter hour Senator Castle said he would be happy to continue for another fifteen minutes—"since you're so well prepared and so well informed." The student interviewer gratefully kept him on the air.

Breakfast was with Forum committee members. He answered questions for a half hour.

A car met him and shuttled him to an old Romanesque-style brick structure, outnumbered, on this campus, by buildings of puckered gray concrete. He was led down a dark hallway, his shoes clopping on red tiles, past bulletin boards bursting with notices on colored paper—*Earn $1,000 from home...Spring break in Cancún...MCAT prep service.* He was handed over to an old professor dressed in tweed who shook his hand loosely and introduced him to the history seminar as a special guest. For today, the class had been turned into a question-and-answer session with "the widely respected junior senator from North Dakota."

At eleven he held a press conference at the student union. General Westmoreland, waiting in the wings, would come in at eleven-thirty to conduct his own press conference. Both were asked if they would consent to a joint press conference at the end of the hour. Senator Castle smiled at General Westmoreland and said, "I'll do whatever my hosts and hostesses want me to do."

The general said it would be preferable to postpone a joint

appearance until the time of their scheduled engagement at seven o'clock.

Lunch was in the student dining hall, at a table reserved for twenty students majoring in political science. The hall hadn't changed much since Reuben's time in Urbana, his single year in law school, for which his grades were now expunged from the record. He had passed through this linoleum-and-concrete palace dozens of times, but never, to his recollection, had he been aware of the special parking lot nearby, made available to visiting VIPs, and certainly he had never been greeted by such a gaggle of fresh-faced nascent politicians. They were hunched forward, the boys' ties dangling precariously close to their bowls of Jell-O, nodding and smiling before he even spoke a word.

In the afternoon, Reuben attended an ROTC class. He declined to answer questions on whether such courses as the one he was participating in should be formally affiliated with a college or figure in its curriculum. "But as a veteran, I'd be glad to attend your drill, and proud to salute the flag." He did both, and gave an impromptu speech about the need to take diplomatic initiatives in dealing with the Soviet Union.

A tea was given by the university president, and Reuben listened with manifest concern to talk about the increasing costs of higher education. He agreed that the federal government would need to extend a more abundant hand.

General Westmoreland had greeted Senator Castle with the deference habitually paid by the military to money-disbursing members of Congress. But he said nothing more than was needed, remarking only that an uncle of his had attended the University of Illinois just after the First World War, and had left a part of his tiny estate to the university. Reuben Castle nodded, along with the others, his appreciation of that deed. "I wish Uncle Sam was as generous as your uncle, General."

The general nodded, and one could discern a smile, at half mast. The president said how glad the university always was to receive in Urbana such important guests, who had so much to say about common concerns.

After the tea, time had been put aside to permit the visitors to rest or shower before dinner. Returned to his room, Reuben went to the telephone. "Anything happening, Susan?"

"Yes. The president's going on the air tonight. Apparently to stick it to Saddam Hussein and call on him to honor the UN resolution."

"Remind me, which one is that?"

"It's 667. Condemns Iraq's violation of Kuwait's borders."

"I'll blame it all on Westy."

"How's it going otherwise?"

"Okay. Nice kids. They keep you busy."

"And they all vote."

Assembly Hall was full. There were placards, but not like the old days, Reuben remarked to Jane Sander, who had stayed with him all day, escorting him to his engagements. "Well, that's an improvement, I guess, Senator."

"I don't know, Jane. Remember, I did my share of protesting. I was one of *them*!"

Jane blushed for giving the impression that she was unaware of this important biographical detail. She made up for it quickly and easily: "You made for a better world, Senator."

• • •

The two principals had individual waiting rooms backstage. The vibrancy of the audience reached them through the stage curtain. A student technician adjusted the loudspeakers. *"Testing one two three."* Silence followed. Finally a voice from the rear of the hall rang out: *"Try four five six."* There was a ripple of laughter, and another student onstage tested the mikes at the lecterns, left and right, by ticking them with a ballpoint pen.

Seated in his waiting room, Reuben was idling over a notepad on his lap when consternation struck. General Westmoreland was not well.

Alex Wholley, the Forum president, came in, wide-eyed. *"He's sick,* Senator. Oh, my God!" He wheeled around. "Be right back."

He was gone five minutes, then reappeared with Jane Sander. "Senator, I don't know what we're going to do. We've sent for an ambulance to take the general to the infirmary. We haven't made any announcements out there. Oh, gee. Oh, *shit!"*

"Listen." Reuben rose from his chair and addressed the two students.

"Here's what we'll do. I'll play the role of the general, affirming Vietnam. And then I'll play my role, critical of the whole thing. There isn't a word General Westmoreland has spoken or written in the last twenty years that I haven't heard, studied, and thought about.

"Alex, you go out center stage. Tell them that there's been a little emergency, but that the views of General Westmoreland will be fully and persuasively presented. I'll come in from backstage, I'll go to his lectern, the general's lectern, and I'll speak for ten minutes. Then you get up and say, 'Now let's hear a different point of view, from our other guest, Senator Reuben Castle.' I'll go to the other lectern and speak for ten minutes. Then I'll ask a couple of questions. And answer them, as he would have answered them. Then he will ask *me* a couple of questions and I'll answer. Then you can take the show to the audience."

It was a striking success. Nobody, in the excited discussions later in the evening, could fault the pleading done on behalf of Westmoreland's position that the war had been just, and justified, a failure at last only because support for it declined.

Senator Castle, bobbing over to the other side of the stage, concluded by saying that the decline in support for the war was a historic demonstration of the viability of the democratic process.

At this the crowd went wild. There was a standing ovation. The chairman reminded the audience that the evening was not over, there would be questions from the floor. The questioner should announce whether his question was intended for Senator Castle or for..."his opponent."

The students all but carried Senator Castle away on their shoulders. The student paper's coverage of the event was widely quoted.

Back in Washington, the senator's whole staff assembled to greet him. He smiled his appreciation. "When I run for reelection, I intend to save my honorable opponent the nuisance of appearing at any of our debates."

CHAPTER 30

South Bend, May 1991

Days before final exams, Justin got word that Professor Lejeune wanted to see him. About what? Justin had submitted a junior thesis on three major philological events in the French language in the twentieth century, a subject to which his grandfather had devoted a substantial part of his academic life. Justin was pleased with his work and sent a Xerox copy to his mother, who would read it with professional care. He could not imagine that the reclusive M. Lejeune would call him in to chat about Justin Durban's ideas on French word changes. He was keenly curious when he stepped into the crowded but orderly little office in the Decio building.

Armand Lejeune was a scholar of solitary, even antisocial, habits ("Professor of Aloofness," one graduate student had labeled him). His interests were in the great, mesmerizing language he taught and reveled in. Lejeune had been born in France and raised there, until midway through World War II. In 1942 his father was martyred when the Nazis got onto the code by which he was transmitting information to the British. No one had ever communicated to his widow the details of his last days. Four weeks after she and twelve-year-old Armand were smuggled out to safety in England, a letter arrived from her husband via Sweden, carefully composed to avoid attracting the attention of the censors. There was a frugal reference to a local celebration of the French national holiday, so he was certainly alive on July 14. But nothing more was ever heard from him, or about him. Madame Lejeune, teaching French and working nights in the French army hospital, raised her boy in London.

Justin had had an earlier experience of the Professor of Aloofness. As a competitor for a place on *The Observer*, he had been randomly assigned to write a profile of the august new chairman of the French department, hired away from Cornell. Justin called on M. Lejeune, hoping for a conversation that would yield readable copy. Lejeune wasn't mute, but he didn't divulge any features of his personal life that might have made Justin's story more interesting. Personal details occasionally emerged, but mostly they served simply as background for the academic accomplishments noted in his curriculum vitae, which the department had sent out.

Lejeune had been hired to head up Notre Dame's French department and hold the Masterson Chair. The French department had been deemed laggard by the proud standards of the humanities division. The dean had available, for distribution to the alumni magazine and to the student and local papers, only the barest curriculum vitae for the bachelor newcomer, which included excerpts from reviews of Lejeune's acclaimed work on French drama. The two volumes on Molière and Corneille were already published. The third, on Racine, was scheduled for 1990. The press release told of the author's six years of schooling in Great Britain, of the master's degree in French literature from Cambridge, followed by eight years as an instructor at the London School of Economics. After that, associate professor at Cambridge, then full professor at Cornell, where he had written his academic volumes on the French dramatists. It surprised some of his colleagues at Cornell that, given his known aversion to social intercourse, Armand Lejeune had accepted the job of department chairman at Notre Dame. "He's going to have to talk to *somebody*," one colleague remarked at coffee after a faculty meeting.

"Yes. Though maybe Armand will figure out a way to do it by mail."

But he had become the active head of a department that offered no fewer than twenty-four courses. A half dozen of these were what Lejeune had been heard to refer to as "delicatessen courses in instrumental French." And in fact they were attended by almost 200 students, many of them bent only on satisfying the undergraduate foreign-language requirements of Notre Dame. These academic conscripts had signed up for first-year and second-year French and would be satisfied if, later in life, they could negotiate a French menu or direct a Paris taxi. That was not the case with Justin Durban and Allard de Minveille. They were both taking courses in French literature, and Allard was especially attracted to French poetry.

What the harried department chairman wanted from young Justin that May afternoon came as an awesome and flattering surprise. He asked Justin to take on, in senior year, the teaching of one section of the first-year course in the French language, French 10ab.

Lejeune spoke to Justin in French, confirming what he had observed upon arriving in South Bend and being pressed for an interview, in fluent French, by the freshman student. Justin's knowledge of the language was that of a native, as one would expect. But the young man had a manner of speaking that attracted attention and conveyed authority.

Justin was eager to answer any questions put to him, but there weren't many. Lejeune was struggling with a very tight budget and an unanticipated student demand for beginning French. He had been left hard up for qualified teachers. Yes, it was unusual to hire an undergraduate as a member of the faculty, but the circumstances were unusual, and here he found himself with access to a twenty-one-year-old with native schooling in the language. Lejeune had established that Durban was a serious student, and that he had earned the esteem of faculty members who had taught and dealt with him.

After a half hour's conversation, Lejeune gave Justin the details: fifty-minute classes, five times a week, fourteen students.

Faculty rank: assistant in instruction. Compensation: $4,200 for the academic year. Justin left Lejeune's office wild with anticipation and delight.

CHAPTER 31

En route to Tallahassee, Florida, January 1991

"Have you evah met this...mayah?" Priscilla Castle still had in her voice the light southern lilt acquired during her Alabama childhood.

"No. I haven't actually met him," Reuben said. "But in that line of work—I mean, being a mayor—he is in category number one, and the award he's giving us is much sought after."

"By whom?"

"Well, by whom do you think, Priscilla? Not by people who want to start animal hospitals."

"Are you against animals today, Reuben? What happened? You discovered they don' vote?"

"Oh, come on, Priscilla." He beckoned to the stewardess for more coffee.

"And I'll have more wine," Priscilla said, motioning with her empty glass.

"So, at the big banquet we are hailed by the mayah as Couple of the Year, and he makes a speech about us. What are *we* supposed to do? Fuck for him? What happened to the other competitors for Couple of the Year? The losers? Didn' fuck to the satisfaction of the mayah?"

"Priscilla, for God's sake. And...keep your voice down. Four jet engines can't compete when you get riled up." The wine and coffee were served.

"Well, okay." She stretched out her legs and tilted back her head, a head that was once famously beautiful. "So I was exaggerating."

"So you were just exercising your dirty little mind."

"So—I had to come along because Couple of the Year is one more step toward the golden prize." She drank her wine. "You might at least bring along some decent wine when you drag me around on these chickenshit missions."

"You don't care if they're chickenshit as long as you have enough booze—"

"Whaddaya mean *enough*?" She laughed. "There isn't enough in the province of Bordeaux—that's Bordeaux, France—to anaesthetize me on one of your Celebrate Reuben trips." Without turning her head to the attendant she extended her hand with the empty glass, as if placing it under a beer tap.

"Well now, Miss America, you had to flit around the country a little in 1973 when you were doing your own campaign. Wherever there was a judge or a likely judge, Miss Colorado was there with her manager—what was his name?"

"You talkin' about Amos?"

"Yes. I'll have to ring him up, ask him how he managed to keep you sober."

But she had begun to cry. Reuben, in the aisle seat as always, tried to calm her. He spoke soothingly. "You were very beautiful, Priscilla."

"*Were* very beautiful?" She sobbed some more, and brought a handkerchief to her face. "*Were* very beautiful! What am I now? *Very* ugly?"

"Oh, come on. You are still very beautiful."

"Do you think so?"

"I know so. Did you see the picture of Miss Florida? It was with the packet sent up by the mayor's office. Anyway, she couldn't hold a candle up against you."

"But she is *seventeen* years youngah. Are you sayin' that makes no difference?"

Reuben considered just giving up. He adjusted first her seat belt and then his own against the turbulence. He smoothed out her pillow. Her left hand went under the tray to his groin. He gave her a sign of life, and then, happily, she was asleep.

CHAPTER 32

Washington, February 1991

Susan Oakeshott got the hot new polling figures. She studied them as an astronomer might study galactic oscillations. Squinting her eyes she could discern little reconfigurations not noticeable to the lay community. She resisted any temptation she might have had, after these deliberations, to act impulsively. To pick up her candidate from the polling floor, or let him down tenderly with a new speech in his mouth or a revised position for, or against, a pending measure. She didn't do that mostly because her candidate was Reuben Castle, and she thought him the smartest man in town on the political beat, capable of picking up his own signals if they were of true consequence.

The question was whether even to let him in on her thinking, when she felt she had identified something worth noting—a discerned weakness, perhaps, that might hamper him in the months ahead. She was keenly conscious that what might strike her as distasteful, or disagreeable, or even offensive, might not strike others in the same way. When she served Adam Benjamin, during his five years in the House of Representatives, she noticed, as he headed into his fourth election campaign, a creeping stiffness of manner. Could it have been that she, Susan, had become more aloof? No no no no. The thing about Susan Oakeshott was that she *never* changed. The skies and the forests and the oceans might change, but not Susan Oakeshott; that was why politicians called on her when the Bureau of Weights and Measures was equivocal. She was as feminine as required indisputably to establish her gender and draw on its attributes. But nothing distracting was added to get in Susan's way, nothing in her dress, nothing in her manner, nothing in her expressions.

On the matter of the stiffness of Congressman Benjamin . . . It had to be he who for some reason had changed. She wondered whether the change reflected his military background. He had, after all, spent four years at West Point, followed by three years in the U.S. Infantry, rising to first lieutenant. He had gone back to civilian life, studying law, and when Susan went to him, in 1975, he was competent as a lawyer and agreeable enough as a citizen, making pleasant way with his constituents in Gary, Indiana. But he was easily intimidated by rank. When the horrible news reached him that the candidate he would be facing in 1980 was a retired general—*a fucking general*, as anyone other than Benjamin would have greeted this development—he visibly lost heart, especially at the prospect of two debates at the University of Indiana. Susan never intimated to anyone her suspicion that Mr. Benjamin's sudden death at forty-four, three months before the election, might have been precipitated by the press conference at which the general had said he proposed to teach "Lieutenant Benjamin" that there was rank to be observed not merely in military but also in civilian life.

Reuben Castle, she often reminded herself, was in many ways the ideal political figure. He was intelligent—not learned, but quick as a light hare—and renowned for his good looks. The earnestness on his face when he was arguing a political position was followed so quickly, so disarmingly, by an affability nearly aggressive, first appeasing, then disarming his critics.

The one problem that now concerned Susan had to do with the merging of Castle's ambition and his self-esteem. The Reuben Castle of 1991 was just about ready to conclude that it was not only conceivable but altogether likely that he would do well in the forthcoming campaign, win the critical primaries, and emerge as the Democratic candidate for president of the United States.

This turn in his thinking was readable, however faintly, in his manner. It's one thing, Susan thought to herself, to exhibit self-confidence of the kind that tells the listener you know you are fighting for a cause that is just. It becomes a little more than that—actually, quite another thing—to give the impression that your cause is just because it is your cause.

How to say that to him? How even to...describe the problem? It had briefly crossed her mind to discuss the matter with Harold Kaltenbach in one of his increasingly frequent telephone calls, but no. Hal had no patience with any talk about his candidate's manner. He wanted to talk about where the candidate should appear, what issues he should stress, whom he should endorse, whose financial aid he should solicit, whose he should grandly—or discreetly—decline. Hal had no time to reflect on, let alone adjudicate, questions that had to do with human temperament. Those matters, if relevant, had been weighed by Kaltenbach before he took a candidate on. They were yesterday's questions, and mustn't interfere with today's priorities.

So, on the phone, Hal moved down his own list of questions for the day. Susan could tell that he was feeling a quiet optimism about the candidacy of Reuben Hardwick Castle.

• • •

It was February, and the invitations to give commencement speeches had begun coming in. Susan was accustomed to these, after ten years of service with Senator Castle. She knew that the issuance of these invitations was governed by three considerations.

(1) Could the sponsoring college, without depreciating the tradition, grant an honorary doctorate to this particular invitee? If the proposed honoree had given a great deal of money to the college, that was always qualifying. Graduating students could understand an honorary degree for the gentleman who had come up with a few million dollars for a new physics lab. But other candidates were judged by other criteria.

(2) Would the proposed honoree do a creditable job delivering the commencement address? There was no question here about Castle's competence. But did he have sufficient status as a figure in public life? Reuben Castle had so far accumulated four doctorates of law (LLD) and four of letters (LittD) during his time in the Senate, but had only twice been asked to be the commencement speaker. However, he was steadily rising to national prominence, his growing reputation fueled by performances like the Westmoreland debate.

(3) Could the college reasonably expect that the honoree would not ask a heavy speaker's fee? That he would settle for expenses, generously conceived? No problem here with Castle. Under Senate rules, senators were not permitted to receive any speaking fees, let alone exorbitant ones.

Susan expected invitations to come in from about a dozen

campuses. The trick was to delay accepting an invitation from lesser folk, pending a crystallization of the larger picture. Two came early: little Haverford, in Pennsylvania, and another small campus nearby, Lafayette. Both were distinguished old colleges, but not front-page news. Susan bought two weeks of time by doing nothing. The invitations just lay there.

Then she would wangle a little more time by asking for precise schedules, "because the senator's agenda is very full this year." Back-and-forth on that could get you another two weeks' delay. By then any heavier hitters should have rolled in.

In the third week of March, the senator received invitations to give commencement talks at the University of North Carolina, the University of Maryland, and Johns Hopkins. Not quite the same as Harvard, Stanford, and Columbia, but pretty good. Have to act now. Time to call Hal.

"Tell you what, Susan. Have one of the people on the staff— Bill Rode would do this okay—write to them and say the senator has been asked by the president to hold a couple of dates (don't say which) to handle West Point or the Naval Academy or the Air Force Academy in case the president can't make it on account of Iraq. He wants a Democrat to make an appearance for bipartisan reasons. So the whole schedule will need to be frozen until—oh, March 24. That way we can give the bigtimers one more week. Susan?"

"Yes, Hal?"

"If things go right, in a few years Reuben will be telling *them* when to hold their commencement exercises!"

The strategy worked, and the last-minute invitation from the University of Pennsylvania was accepted. That monopolized one Saturday, and left the senator free to accept a lesser academic patron the Saturday before Philadelphia, and another the Saturday after.

It was always a happy development when Priscilla gave word that she did not wish to go along on a particular speaking trip. But the office could never count on that. Sometimes she insisted on going. And then what? The University of Pennsylvania had expressed itself as hoping very much that Mrs. Castle would accompany the senator and perhaps even say a few words at the banquet the night before the commencement exercises. There was nothing to be done when that happened; no interposition was thinkable. "It's always possible, Bill," Susan offered hope to the nervous Bill Rode, "that Priscilla won't feel up to it."

"Sure. That can happen. I remember the University of Texas last year, no problem."

"Yes. No problem. The problem comes if she *does* feel like going."

"We'll just have to hope and pray. How did she react when you told her they wanted her to say something at the banquet?"

"She said that would be good. She'd been used to giving little speeches going back to when she was nineteen years old."

"And now she's running for Miss First Lady."

"Quiet. We don't allow those words to be spoken. The main event is Senator Castle, receiving an honorary degree and giving a nonpartisan talk on the Gulf War and the need to contain Saddam Hussein."

"Yes. Contain Saddam and contain Priscilla."

CHAPTER 33

Boulder, June 1991

At the beginning of summer vacation, preparing for senior year at Notre Dame, Justin set out to save one thousand dollars. If he succeeded, his mother, serving as trustee, would invade his grandfather's fund to the tune of a second thousand dollars. And the money would get Justin a sturdy used car.

As a senior at Notre Dame, he was authorized to keep a car on campus. It would be the fulfillment of a dream, having his own car. He told his mother, and told Amy, and told Alice Robbins, Paul's mother, what good deeds he might perform, having his own car.

It was very hard work at the Balthasar Construction Company, but the pay was good, eight dollars an hour, overtime after forty hours, and a supplementary twenty-five percent for work done on Saturdays and Sundays.

Justin began by helping to haul heavy materials. "Maman, I figure today by noon—that's starting at six-thirty—I had transported four tons, presque quatre mille kilos, of cement from the warehouse onto trucks. We were given a five-minute break at the end of every hour. Maman, I think maybe I should take up smoking cigarettes. That's what the men mostly do during those breaks."

"That would be quite silly. Cigarettes are very expensive now. It would be the equivalent of taking away—oh, ten, fifteen percent from your salary."

"I wouldn't like that."

"Nor would your lungs."

"They'll invent something for lungs before I get old."

"Justin, you stop right now, close your eyes, and say a prayer. Just say, 'Je m'excuse, mon Seigneur, de ma bêtise.' "

"All right." He held up his hand. "Don't interrupt me while I'm praying." He lowered his hand after a few seconds. "Done." He indicated that he had made amends with his maker for his foolishness in presuming a cure around the corner. Then he winked. "Well, okay. I said we could skip lung cancer— and settle for a cure for venereal disease." He roared with laughter.

Henrietta just smiled and turned back to the catalogue she was looking through. "Have you decided what sort of automobile you'll get?"

"I've been thinking a lot about that, and trying to decide whether I should buy it here or in South Bend. I have a friend at college, Jimmy—his family lives in South Bend, and he's going to clip ads from the papers giving prices, and I can compare them with prices here. Maman, I think I will end up with a Ford. Or maybe a Chevrolet."

"And you have promised that you will wear a seat belt at all times. And that—complètement défendu!—you will never drive if you have had anything to drink."

"Students aren't allowed to drink on campus. So when would I be drinking?"

Henri didn't even smile at the effrontery.

• • •

He left, in his brand-new old car, a full week before classes began at Notre Dame. He said he was going to do a few days' fishing with his friend Mike O'Brien, who knew just where to go.

Henri asked, "Where is Mike O'Brien from?"

"You mean hometown? I don't know. But he's out of state, I know that." He smiled at his mother. "Don't worry. I'll send you a postcard."

She helped him pack the car, and they embraced. Although he was beginning his fourth year at Notre Dame, Henri still had not got used to saying good-bye to her son.

CHAPTER 34

Grand Forks, September 1991

Justin's destination was not South Bend but Grand Forks. He had established that the University of North Dakota's fall semester began a week before Notre Dame's.

After paying for the car, he was short on funds. He didn't want to spend money on motels and was prepared to use his tent, neatly packed in the trunk along with his fishing rod and his shotgun. But before pitching his tent somewhere outside the city, he decided to see if there was anything around in the way of native hospitality. He sought out the office of the *Dakota Student*, where he displayed, not without a trace of pride, his press card, identifying him as a junior editor of the Notre Dame *Observer*. He was a fellow journalist.

The girl on duty was pleasant and inclined to be helpful. "I'm doing a story on your junior senator," Justin told her, "focusing on his time at UND. Castle may be going big-time. Meanwhile I have a practical question: is there any chance of getting a dormitory room so I don't have to pay for a motel?"

The editor was solicitous. "Hm. Let's see. Hm. For how long?"

"Maybe three, four days. Maybe less."

"Harold Burton has a room at Alpha Chi, and he's going

to be a week late getting back from Spain. I know, because he called and asked me to straighten it out with the dean. I'm sure he wouldn't mind if you used his room. He's that kind of a guy."

"That would be great. Can you show me where? Then I'll come back and start my research on the senator right here."

"Sure. But all we have is back issues, that kind of thing. We don't keep story files." She extended her hand. "I'm Judy, by the way. I'm a journalism major, and a junior. And I hold the fort at the *Student* apart from press days. We publish twice a week, Tuesday and Friday."

An hour later, Justin was back, carrying his laptop. He started to track down references to Reuben Castle. There were a great many, dating back to his election to the staff as a junior editor in 1967.

Justin started reading Castle's columns. They concentrated heavily on the war, and on the impending deployment of the Sentinel missiles in North Dakota. Justin got a kick out of the Zap campaign.

After a while he picked up the phone and called Judy's extension. "Is there anybody around here who was at UND when Castle was?"

"That was when?"

"That was... 1966 to 1970."

"I don't know, not for sure. Maybe Maria Cervantes was here back then. You want her phone number? She's dean of students."

Justin made the call.

• • •

Maria Cervantes proved to be a portly woman who wore glasses low on her nose. Outside her navy blue blouse a gold chain hung, a gold sorority pin suspended from it. She inquired matter-of-factly about Justin's mission. "I used to be on the *Dakota Student*, so I'm disposed to be hospitable to student reporters. They usually don't know enough," she smiled, "to do any harm."

"Ma'am, did you by any chance know Reuben Castle?"

"I certainly did. We competed together to join the staff of the *Student*. Then we competed for the office of editor in chief. He won, though Eric Monsanto gave him a run for his money. But Eric settled for business manager."

"Castle was pretty successful, right, ma'am?"

"Oh, yes. He won just about everything he contended for, including chairman of the Student Council."

"Did he have a girlfriend?"

Maria Cervantes drew back for a moment. "Every male student has a girlfriend."

"Anybody you knew?"

"Yes. Henrietta. A lovely girl."

"*Henrietta?*"

"Yes. Don't remember her last name. I tell you what, Justin. If you really want to get into the story of Reuben twenty years ago, why don't you go see Eric Monsanto? He's here in town, a lawyer, family firm. Nice guy. He and Reuben were just like that—best friends. If you like, I'll call him up from right here. He'll give you a few minutes, I'm sure."

Eric Monsanto did more than that. He told Maria to invite

Justin to come to his house for a drink. Eric's wife and children were away, and his office work would not detain him.

Her hand over the receiver, Maria conveyed the invitation. Justin nodded acceptance, and at six-fifteen he made his way to 18 Edgewater Road. He walked to the front door of the imposing brick house and rang the doorbell. A trim, dark-haired man opened the door. He stared hard at Justin for a moment and then invited him in and, with a friendly smile, offered him a chair.

"Do you drink?"

"A beer would be great, sir."

Justin looked about the large wood-paneled room with all the photographs. He squinted his eyes and adjusted his glasses. Might one of those pictures have Reuben Castle in it?

He accepted the beer, and spoke engagingly, if, after the second beer, a little discursively—he was in no hurry to get back to Alpha Chi—about life at South Bend and his anxiety to turn in a good story on Castle for the first fall issue of *The Observer.* "A lot of people think Senator Castle is going to run for president next year. Have you stayed in touch?"

"Well, sort of. When he went into the army, I went into the navy, and there wasn't much communication between the two services. Then, as your research no doubt tells you, Reuben— Senator Castle—went to law school at Urbana. I went to Harvard. And of course he didn't stay with the law. The call of politics!"

"Sir, are you a Democratic member— Sorry. I mean, are you involved in the senator's election campaigns?"

"Oh, no. I...have loved Reuben dearly, but I'm a Republican, so he knows not to come around at election time."

"Did you spend a lot of time together when you were under-graduates? I know you were both on the newspaper, but—socially?"

"Oh, yes. We were very close."

"Did he have a steady girlfriend?"

Monsanto's hesitation was noticeable. "Yes. But that was back then, and as we both know, he is married, I hope happily—"

"You don't know Miss America? I mean, Mrs. Castle?"

"We've just met, that's all. They don't spend much time in this neck of the woods."

"His college girlfriend, are you in touch with her?"

"No. Not at all. She went to Paris in senior year to be with her father. Her name was Leborcier. She was a Canadian—I mean, she was born in Canada. In Letellier—that's just north of here a stretch. In fact she went to the convent school in Letellier as a girl. . . . No, I don't know what happened."

Justin turned away.

"Looking for the washroom?"

Justin shook his head.

His host went and got himself another drink and, for Justin, another beer. "How long are you going to be in town? If you'll be here Friday, you can come with me for a little fishing. I have a nice duck blind over at Devil's Lake where we could spend the night."

CHAPTER 35

Letellier, September 1991

At the second crossroads in Letellier, Justin looked hard at the signpost and took the westerly road, arriving a few minutes later at Saint Joseph's Convent. It was nearly eleven-thirty. He rang the bell and a nun emerged.

"May I come in, Sister?"

"Yes, young man." She closed the door and led him into a neat anteroom with faded curtains and slipcovers.

"Sister, I am trying to find information about someone who was a student at the convent school here in the '50s."

"What is her name? And what is your business?"

"Her name is Henrietta Leborcier. Mine is Justin Durban. I'm a student at Notre Dame, but I come from Grand Forks, and this summer I've been working for a lawyer named Eric Monsanto." He reached into his shirt pocket and brought out the card Monsanto had given him the night before.

The sister glanced at the card and returned it.

Justin went on without waiting for her to speak. "We are trying to locate Ms. Leborcier because there is a gift, a small legacy from someone who knew her at the University of North Dakota. Mr. Monsanto was a friend of hers back then, though he has lost touch with her, and he says she attended school at the convent here. In fact she was born in Letellier."

"You may not be aware that our school is closed. It merged with one in Montreal."

"So you have no records here, Sister?"

"We have some things. If you will accompany me, we can go to the student index file." She rose and walked unevenly down the high-ceilinged, faded hallway, taking out her key ring to open a door.

"This was the mother superior's office."

Inside, she lifted a tray down from a shelf overhead. "Leborcier." She withdrew a card. "Henrietta Leborcier. Born 1948 in Letellier. Daughter of Raymond and Esther Leborcier. Baptized and confirmed at Saint Anne's by Father François Lully."

She raised her head. "God bless him, he is an old man now, but he still writes to us regularly."

"He is no longer in Letellier?"

"No. He was moved to a parish in Winnipeg some years ago, and he has since retired. The current pastor is Father Daniel."

"Do you think he'd let me look at the parish records?"

"I'm sure he would. Do you know Letellier at all? No? Well, drive back the way you came, until you get to First Avenue—that's the main street, running north–south. Turn left onto First Avenue, and you'll soon come to Saint Anne's." Justin asked if he might see the Saint Joseph chapel.

"Of course, just come with me."

She opened the vaulted wooden door. There was stained glass in Victorian effusion behind the altar at the far end. Then came the nuns' pews. In the front were the pews of the girls. Three rows on his left, facing three rows on his right. He could imagine as many as a hundred girls seated, or kneeling, there. He knelt at the prie-dieu in the vestibule and uttered a brief but earnest prayer to Saint Justin Martyr to guide him.

At Saint Anne's, he rang the bell at the rectory. "Is Father Daniel in?" he asked the woman who opened the door.

"Yes. But he is resting. What can I do for you, young man?"

"I need to speak to him. I was sent here by the sister at Saint Joseph's."

He heard a man's voice in the back. "Let him in, Claudette. I am fully awake."

Justin entered the dusky living room. A middle-aged man in shirtsleeves took his hand and beckoned him to the sofa.

"I am Justin Durban from Grand Forks, Father. I am a student at Notre Dame, but this summer I've been working for Mr. Eric Monsanto. I am going to be a lawyer myself." He handed the priest Monsanto's card.

"What can I do for you, Justin, if you'll permit me to use your Christian name—at least until you become a judge!"

"Thank you. By all means, Father. We are trying to locate a woman named Henrietta Leborcier. There is a legacy from someone who was a friend of hers at the University of North Dakota. Mr. Monsanto knew she had attended school at the convent here. I went to Saint Joseph's, and there is a record of her attendance, from 1953 to 1959, and again in 1962, but nothing more. No record of relatives in the area or anything like that. The sister suggested I go to you."

"Well, let's see. Father Lully would have been the pastor throughout that time, but for myself I don't recall ever hearing the name Leborcier. We'll see if there is anything here. We do not keep a general directory of parishioners, but we have a record of baptisms, first communions, confirmations, weddings, and funerals. Come into my study."

He brought down onto a long table covered with green felt three heavy leather-bound volumes. "Here are books that reach back to the 1940s. Each volume holds records for about ten years. Why don't you just sit down and examine them? I wish I could say that there was some sort of alphabetized index. Can I have Claudette bring you a cup of tea?"

Justin's face brightened. "Father, could I be very rude? I wonder if you have a cookie, or an apple? I did not stop for lunch."

"Of course!"

Claudette was in the room, dusting. And listening. "I'll fetch something, Father."

A few minutes later Justin was munching a cookie as he turned the pages, page after page, without finding "Leborcier."

"All baptisms would be recorded, Father?"

"In principle, though sometimes if we're very busy we might slip up. You said that Saint Joseph's records her as having been baptized here?"

"Yes, but they didn't have a date. We're just assuming it would have been in 1948 or '49, since she was born in September 1948."

"Well, just keep looking, Justin. That's what lawyers have to do much of the time."

Justin began to wonder why he was turning pages that took

him into the 1960s, but he resolved to continue until he had at least finished the third volume.

He had reached November 1969. On the second page for the month, he read, "*November 18. Married. Reuben Hardwick Castle, Henrietta Seringhaus Leborcier.*"

His eyes froze, and his heart stopped.

The two signatures were there. He recognized his mother's script. He was unfamiliar with that of...his father. With his right hand he reached for his pocket camera and snapped a picture.

He paused a good while. Then: "Father, where would the actual wedding certificate be?"

"It is taken away by the principals. We have just these registry notations. Of course, the civil record, the signed marriage license, would have been sent up to Winnipeg, to the Vital Statistics Agency. Perhaps they would have a mailing address, you are wondering? But surely those addresses would be obsolete. This was more than twenty years ago."

"Thank you, Father, but I think with what I have here—what I have written down—we can track her current address." He thought to add a touch of drama. "If she is still living, of course."

"Would you care for more cookies? Or you could have an apple."

"Thank you so much." Justin extended his hand to Father Daniel and nodded to thank Claudette, who was busy mending a book.

It was more than an hour to Grand Forks. Nightfall. He considered going to Mr. Monsanto, but as he approached the highway exit, he decided to keep it all to himself. *Keep it all to himself?* Bewilderment overcame him. Why would...How could...He improvised answers to his questions, and discarded them. Ten miles beyond Grand Forks he impulsively pulled over to the shoulder thinking, momentarily, of returning to Mr. Monsanto after all. But restlessness took over, and the impulse to move, to drive the car, to push himself. To sleep was out of the question. He set out for South Bend.

But that was 700 miles away. Saint Paul was in the right direction. He reached the outskirts of the city at two in the morning, and pulled in at a motel and slept deeply.

CHAPTER 36

Grand Forks, September 1991

Eric Monsanto woke up at midnight, restless. His mind trained on the young man who had visited him that evening. Justin Durban.

"Duhrbahn," he had pronounced his surname—French style. Monsanto wondered what the French connection was. He could hardly supply such details, having no knowledge of his own about the visitor. He had agreed to speak with the kid—acting instinctively. He would agree, as a matter of course, to meet with any young man or woman who was on a journalistic assignment. Why should he know more about his visitor than just that—that he was a student journalist at Notre Dame? That hardly made Eric Monsanto an expert on young Justin Durban. Without even pausing in his thought stream, he said to himself out loud, tapping his middle finger adamantly on his head, *"That boy is the son of Reuben Castle."*

Could he be mistaken?

No. Not possible. The looks, the build, the blondness, the smile—even the manner. Though Reuben was more aggressive. Reuben Castle simply wanted—always—to win; prevail; get in there first. This kid was less direct than his father would have been, engaging at age twenty-one in an interview with a stranger. But the intense focus was the same.

Reuben Castle. Mix in Henrietta Leborcier—so pretty, blue-eyed, tall, appealing, adoring—and you had Justin Durban.

Rico Monsanto had spent a fair amount of time worrying about Henri, back in senior year at UND. He had had that ugly—and revealing—scene with Reuben at the Hop See. It was then that the estrangement came. Not formally—they continued to work together on the *Dakota Student*, and Eric continued to serve on the Student Council, of which Reuben was chairman. No, not formally, but essentially.

Eric had at first been disappointed and hurt that Henrietta hadn't written to him again from Paris. There had been only the solitary letter from her, professing concern for Reuben, which had led to the confrontation at the Hop See. That night, back at home, he wrote to Henri, giving her the news, that Reuben had decided...to step away, to abandon Henri and, of course, the child.

But when he thought about it, Eric could understand Henri's decision to sever ties with everyone at the university, even— maybe especially—Reuben's closest friend, himself. He could understand her finding it embarrassing to stay in touch with him, the single person who knew the whole story of the romance. Eric Monsanto was the only other person in Grand Forks who knew, when she pulled away and went to Paris, that Henri was pregnant.

• • •

Eric knew almost nothing about young Justin Durban—
only that he was evidently a student at Notre Dame and an
editor on the student paper. Whatever that paper was called—
he forgot. Eric closed his eyes and thought back to the fall of
1969. More than twenty years ago. The grown-up kid who had
called on him this evening was *surely* the child of the duck-
blind liaison. The child, Rico reflected, that Henri had refused
to abort. He forced his memory back to the details of that
harried week in late October and early November. He—good
old Rico—had been conscripted to carry messages back and
forth. It was he, at Reuben's urgent request, who sped off
to Minneapolis to interview the kind, efficient doctor who
would perform the operation discreetly, and then returned
to Grand Forks and described the procedure to Henrietta. For
his pains Henrietta had professed shock that Rico would even
suggest so obscene an idea: she would not even discuss the
matter. It was to Rico that Henri then confided that what
she wished was to be married—by a priest. By her family priest.
It was Rico who had done the legal research. In Manitoba,
he told her, the application for a marriage license had to be
filed at least twenty-four hours before the license could be
issued.

That flurry had gone on for a week, culminating in the dinner the three undergraduates shared, a bottle of wine discreetly
concealed by a napkin. Eric remembered Reuben telling Henri,
his voice low but easily heard, how much he loved her. She had
replied that she loved him deeply and wanted a lifetime with
him. The appropriate plan immediately suggested itself: she
would go to Paris, continue her college work, have the child
there, and stay with her father until Reuben had graduated. She

said she had an idea or two and would talk to both of them about it in just a few days.

But she didn't do so.

One week later, after a few beers, Reuben said something about having gone with Henri to Letellier, but he clammed up when Rico started to ask questions.

Now, twenty-two years later, this...young man comes to Grand Forks. What was he up to?

At his office early, Eric set out to confirm, or dispel, his suspicions.

His resources for finding people were considerable. He had spent professional time tracking down elusive boys and girls, men and women, grandfathers and grandmothers, establishing whether they were alive or dead, verifying true identities. Sometimes he was acting as a defense attorney, shielding his client from misidentification. More often his responsibility was to establish which of several claimants was entitled to a bequest in a will.

His leads in today's investigation would be enough—provided the young man had told the truth about his name and where he was going to school.

Eric telephoned one of the sleuths he frequently used. He found Nick Finlay at his office in Chicago.

"The guy I want looked into, he has to have been born in Paris. I mean, if he is who I think he is. Because we know the mother went to Paris to stay with her father when the child came. And he would have been born in June 1970."

"Is that a date you're assuming?"

"Well, I have a pretty good idea of it, Nick, unless the mother decided to establish a new birth cycle. I mean, I know—like for sure—when the pregnancy began, which was September 1969. Add nine months, and you get June 1970."

"And the kid—"

"We don't have to call him that, Nick. He told me his name. Justin. Justin Durban. If he lied about that, then we have a real investigation ahead of us. But say he *is* Justin Durban. And say he is at Notre Dame. And say he's on the staff of the student newspaper—those leads should get you started."

"Right. I'll get back to you when I have something."

The fall semester at Notre Dame hadn't yet begun, and members of the university administration were hard to reach. So it was the following week before Finlay accomplished his search of the admissions data and called back.

"Yep. That's him. Born in Paris, May 6, 1970. He lives with his mother in Boulder, Colorado. She's a librarian—her name is Henrietta Leborcier Durban. The student's home address is the same as his mother's, 7 Allenton Place, Apartment 7A."

What would he do now? Eric asked himself.

CHAPTER 37

Boulder, September 1991

Amy Parrish dropped by her own house to change clothes and then drove to Henrietta's apartment for dinner. "Sorry about the delay," she said. "John has the new issue of *Auto News*, and the new Buick is on the cover, and dear John is transported."

"Well," Henri said, "I'm glad you haven't transported John here tonight. My interest in Buick cars is limited. I told you that Justin wound up choosing a Chevrolet?"

"You told me that once, maybe twice. Justin told me about ten times. He was crestfallen that he couldn't buy a Buick."

"You mean John was crestfallen." Henri flipped open the current issue of *Time* magazine to an ad for General Motors. "Justin couldn't buy much of a Buick for two thousand dollars."

"That was his limit?"

"Yes. And, Amy, did he tell you he earned half of that himself? The hard way—hard labor on a construction site. If he ends up as a librarian lugging books, maybe he'll figure he had good training while earning the money to buy the car."

As Henri went into the kitchen, Amy fiddled with the television dial and sipped from her glass of wine. After a few minutes she called out, "You weren't supposed to come up with anything fancy for dinner."

"I haven't. But I'm not going to give you a tuna-fish sandwich."

"Oh? I like tuna fish. Especially cheap tuna fish. Or is all tuna fish cheap?"

Henrietta came back to join her while the oven did its work. She approached her own assignment. "Amy, you knew that I was born in Canada?"

"Sûrement, madame."

"In a little town in southern Manitoba, Letellier. My mother married and conceived her baby—conceived me—there, in Letellier. She was a graduate of Saint Joseph's, the convent school in Letellier, and she sent me there for my early schooling. The mother superior at Saint Joseph's had been like a mother to her."

"Well," said Amy with feigned zest. "Next time I'm in Manitoba I'll make sure to visit Letellier." She stopped suddenly. The subject being skirted was obviously no laughing matter for Henrietta.

"You know that Justin drove off ten days ago?"

"Yes, dear Henri. And I've missed him sorely. Since age fifteen, whenever he would come to visit Allan, he'd make sure to say hello to me. Often he'd seek me out to tell me a risqué joke."

Henri attempted a smile. "He told me he was leaving early in order to go fishing with a friend for a week before the term began."

"That sounds pretty innocent. Has he sent you a fish?"

"No. But he sent me this." She lifted it from the tray. "A postcard mailed from Letellier."

Amy began to take careful interest. "What does he say?"

"He wrote, 'Joli village, Maman, tu devrais le connaître!' Do you understand that?"

"Yes. . . . So he was sightseeing in what used to be your part of the world. I mean, your mother's part of the world—"

"Actually, my part of the world, too. I grew up there until my mother died and my father took me to France. And I went back to Letellier once when I was in college. I went there in 1969 to be married."

Amy spoke slowly now. "You never told me about your marriage with—I don't even know what Lieutenant Durban's first name was."

"Lieutenant Durban never existed. I made up that name when I reached Paris. It was easier to handle Father doing it that way. So of course the child was named Durban. The story I gave out, on which I never elaborated, was that the hypothetical Lieutenant Durban—'Stephen' Durban, by the way—was killed in Vietnam in late April 1970, just before Justin was born."

"Henri. You are telling me that you married someone *else* in Letellier?"

"Hardly 'someone else.' There was only him. Lui seulement."

Amy put down her glass, got up from her chair, and sat down on the sofa next to Henri. "Do you want to tell me all about it, darling?"

"I think so. It's got to be that Justin now knows. He wouldn't have written a message like that otherwise—about Letellier, and how I should go see it. He obviously knows."

"And now I'm to know. Trust me, Henri."

"I do." She picked up her handkerchief.

CHAPTER 38

Washington, September 1991

Reuben sat alone in his office. The letter on his desk was open. It was quaintly direct, almost informal. It sounded like the Rico Monsanto of old, not like Eric Monsanto, JD, counselor at law.

Reuben always greeted Eric amicably when they came upon each other. But such encounters were infrequent, usually at meetings of solid North Dakotans pursuing nonpartisan goals. Eric was on the Northeast Regional Environmental Committee, and Reuben was a member of it, ex officio. There were thirty members, and they had convened in Fargo as recently as last spring. He searched his memory for any personal exchanges he might have had with Rico then, but couldn't come up with anything of interest.

Not quite right, he corrected himself. He had asked after the health of Eric's mother. He couldn't remember what Eric had replied, but he did remember that the conversation was brief, as they filed off for duty at their preassigned seats around the table.

But this. All of a sudden this letter.

He picked it up again.

Dear Reuben:

I have a client to whom I cannot respond properly without first consulting you.

Did you, as I have been given to believe, marry Henrietta Leborcier? If so, when and where did you divorce?

Yours,

Eric

Reuben stared at the tips of his fingers. What, actually, had he done at that old-fashioned rectory, other than try to appease Henri? Henri was truly adorable. *We lost together our cherry / So be merry, dear Henri, be merry.* He remembered murmuring that, nestled in the bedroll, the candle in the corner, sheathed by its glass cylinder, giving out dim illumination, the music from Eric's portable cassette player seeping its melodies through the partition. Above all, he remembered the smile on her face. He'd have consented, that night, to be Henri's slave for ten lifetimes.

He didn't know then that his ejaculate had burrowed down into her ovum. Or had it? Perhaps it was the load from the second engagement—was that at two in the morning? Or conceivably the conception had taken place at the third spasm, at five in the morning, when there was nothing, no candlelight, no daylight, no music from Eric, just her soft flesh and her kisses and her hands stroking his manhood, which came quickly alive.

But now he needed to act. He could delay a few days in replying to Eric, but not much longer. The envelope was marked "Personal from Rico," and Beatrice had dutifully passed it along, unopened. He would not want to dictate a reply, even in Aesopian language. The best thing to do was nothing. That was often the best thing for a senator to do—not to reply until ready. But he knew he had to get ready. He had eventually to reply. And there were things he needed to do first.

How would he put it?

Carefully. To which end he invited Bill Rode for a "working supper."

"Bring your notebook," he said in the presence of Susan.

They met at the little bistro on M Street. They shared a bottle of wine. The junior staff addressed him as "Senator Castle," but he had told Rode to call him Reuben when outside the office, as the senior staff did. Rode said he would be happy to "try to do it" but couldn't guarantee success. "You've been Senator Castle ever since I met you senior year, when you talked at UVA—a hell of a talk...Reuben."

This evening, once they had placed their orders, Reuben started right in: "I've got a personal problem. There was a girl. One of those...things that happen at college. But this girl got carried away and talked me into driving to Canada with her and going through some session with a priest there. The problem is, some people, if they got wind of it, would say that there was a marriage performed. Of course there was no such thing. But what I need to know—Bill, I trust you, and this is in great confidence—is what the parish records show about this, about me and the girl."

Bill nodded gravely. "You want me to go find out?"

"Yes. Fly to Grand Forks, via Minneapolis. Rent a car. Drive to a town called Letellier, a dozen miles north of the Canadian border. Call on the parish priest—there's only one Catholic church there, I'm sure. It's a very small town. Give your name as Bill Thomas. You're doing research for a thesis and you need to look at the parish records. Parish records are generally available to the public, as far as I can figure out. The priest is not going to say they're private. Look to see if there is any record of a marriage ceremony in mid-November 1969."

"Just look for your name?"

Reuben paused. *Might he have been foresighted enough to use a different name?*

"My name. Or the name Henrietta Leborcier."

Bill Rode wrote the name in his notebook. "Should I call you long-distance from there, Reuben?"

"Yes. Use my private line"—he scratched a number on a paper napkin. "If I don't answer, try again at three P.M. I'll make it a point—we're talking about day after tomorrow"—he made a note in his appointment book—"I'll make it a point to be there. No credit cards." He removed $300 from his wallet. "Almost certainly a wild-goose chase. Priscilla is the only girl I ever married. But you never know what they'll come up with. Bastards!"

They finished the wine.

CHAPTER 39

Washington, September 1991

At three-fifteen Reuben put down the telephone. Was there anything else Bill Rode should do?

"No. I'm remembering now. It was kind of a lark. Fraternity stunt. The...page you looked at—loose-leaf, or part of a bound volume?"

"Bound volume, sir."

"Any fuss about seeing it?"

"No. But the priest said somebody was there just a couple of weeks ago looking for the same thing."

"*A couple of weeks ago!*...What do you mean, looking for the same thing?"

"The guy was looking for Leborcier."

"He said it was a guy?"

"Hm, no, he didn't, Senator. He just said *somebody*. Anything else you want me to do, sir?"

"No. Beyond keeping your mouth shut. You know, Bill, what people can do. It was nothing. I'll call the guy who was head of the fraternity back then. He'll probably know where the girl is. Forget it, come on back. But—"

"Yes, boss?"

"I'm thinking. Do you have a cell phone with you?"

"Sure."

"Okay, then give me the number, and stay where you are until I call you back. I've got to sort some things out."

Forget it!

Reuben Castle needed a lawyer. A Canadian lawyer. Shee-yit!

The lawyer would need to be told certain things. Well, lawyers were meant to keep secrets—but he wanted not just *any* lawyer.

He thought hard.

Should he call Eric? Eric would have no trouble finding a lawyer in Winnipeg, a hundred miles way. But then Eric would be in on the whole story, the whole thing. But maybe he's already in on it? He asks me if I married Henri. And if so, when did I divorce her. Jesus Christ. No. Better not call Monsanto till I have everything looked into that I want to look into. Who the hell—

Of course! The U.S. ambassador. Reuben got his name and phone number from Harry, his young staff researcher. He put in a call.

A half hour later he had three names. Three Winnipeg attorneys, all of them "distinguished."

He thought for a moment, thought of the implications in the situation. . . . *Reuben*—he sometimes addressed himself by name in his thoughts, when pondering vexed questions—*Reuben, this is a big one. You'd better handle it yourself.* He called Harry back in. Harry did travel research as well as other research. "Harry, I need to fly to Winnipeg. Tell me how to do that. Day after tomorrow."

He then started down the list of lawyers.

Number one was away.

Reuben began to give the operator the next name on the ambassador's list but suddenly took thought.

Three distinguished lawyers.

That wasn't exactly what he was looking for, come to think of it.

Reuben, what you want is a hard-ass lawyer.

Rode would find the right man. Reuben called Rode on his cell phone. "Bill, I'm looking for a tough lawyer in Winnipeg, one who has the reputation—you know. For getting things done. Call somebody at the newspaper. Find out who is the lawyer that people...that people in serious trouble get in touch with when they want...well, you know, difficult things to get done."

"I know what you mean, Senator. There's always at least one of those in every major city. I'll get back to you."

An hour later Reuben was put though to Henry Griswold. Meanwhile Harry had come in bringing a sheet with flight numbers and times.

Reuben nodded, and Harry left the room. "Mr. Griswold? I'm United States Senator Reuben Castle and I need to consult with an attorney about the Manitoba marriage law. Is that something you are familiar with?"

"Certainly. Is it a question I can handle over the phone?"

"Well, I'd rather discuss it with you in person. I can be in

Winnipeg tomorrow at"—he looked down at Harry's sheet—
"two-thirty. I mean, at the airport at two-thirty. Two-thirty
plus whatever time it takes a taxi—...No, I appreciate that, but
I wouldn't want to put you out of the way. I would rather meet
you in a hotel room than in your office. What's *the* hotel in
Winnipeg?...The Fairmont? Good. What you can do for me is
book me a room there. This is personal; I am not going on
government business. We'll think then of four o'clock?"

He started to phone Jim Stannard, North Dakota's sole congressman. They had an agreement, not often invoked but sometimes very useful. By prearrangement, Stannard, an old personal
friend, would call Reuben asking him to do Jim "a huge favor"
and substitute for him as a "speaker"..."eulogist"..."debater"
in Atlanta...San Antonio...Salt Lake City—or Winnipeg, this
time around. That disposed of the Priscilla problem and often,
even, of the problem of Susan, though it was usually just plain
easier to proceed with life on the understanding that Susan
Oakeshott knew everything, including the names of the ladies
with whom Jim Stannard arranged emergency meetings.

But he didn't want Susan to know about this...engagement.
All he would tell her was that he was taking a couple of days off
to do some duck hunting near Winnipeg with an old buddy from
North Dakota.

CHAPTER 40

Washington, September 1991

By now Harold Kaltenbach didn't care if he was spotted in the company of Reuben Castle. The hand of Kaltenbach was already visible to all the major Democratic players who could see, if not in the dark, then in very little light: the Kaltenbach group was lining up behind Castle for President.

Accordingly, this next engagement to confer with Castle was made not in some remote corner of South Carolina, or on a boat, but at Kaltenbach's suite at the Jefferson Hotel. It was September, the morning of a day quite beautiful, with that cool taste of fall ahead, but not yet overpowering the southern balminess of the District of Columbia.

Riding in the elevator with Reuben, Susan Oakeshott wondered whether Hal Kaltenbach ever noticed the weather. Perhaps if he was snowed in in Omaha. What would such a man, so purposive in all matters, do when such a thing happened? Well, she reasoned, he would retreat to whatever shelter he had emerged from and do his work on the telephone.

Susan had brought along, as instructed to do, her appointment book, and also the thick notebook in which she kept the names, telephone numbers, and addresses—plus other relevant details—of all those who had crossed paths with Reuben Castle.

Kaltenbach was dressed in a blue gabardine suit, a soft white shirt, and a blue-and-yellow tie with, as always, the tiepin "1950." That was the year the University of Nebraska won the conference title. All-American Harold Kaltenbach III was the running back.

There was coffee in the handsome suite's well-stocked bar. Kaltenbach sat behind a mahogany coffee table. Reuben and Susan shared a large sofa, a long low table in reach of them both.

Harold chatted for a few minutes about the rapidly changing scene in Iraq. The United States' failure to apprehend Saddam Hussein and its failure to support the freedom movement of the Kurds were seeds of a considerable political offensive against the Republican establishment. "We need to put it just right, find the right language. We mustn't sound like we're regretting the whole Gulf operation. This is an opportunity for you."

Reuben looked up. "What it is is failed leadership. Can't we call it that?"

"Sure we can call it that. The listener has to be left thinking, 'It was a good idea, we did it well going in, but now we've screwed up—because we don't have the right people there to make the decisions.'"

"That's the general idea. Work on the language, Reuben."

Kaltenbach turned then to concrete questions. "The main thing we're here to settle is when to make the announcement that you're running for president, and where to make it."

"It has to be in Fargo, doesn't it, Hal?"

"That would be nice, and it would be traditional, but we shouldn't think of it as an iron rule. Going back, Reagan announced in Washington, though Los Angeles would have been more the homeboy place to do it. George McGovern is the most relevant precedent where you are concerned, and he announced from Sioux Falls. Jimmy Carter announced from Atlanta. Jerry Ford was in the White House, and obviously announced from there. Nixon announced from California. Johnson was in the White House in 1964, but when he announced in 1960, he did it in Texas. JFK announced in Washington.

"Television makes the venue somehow arbitrary. You could announce from a submarine. Ha-ha. What it comes down to is whether you have more to gain from your odd-state connection or more to lose by drawing attention to it. We're in this for 'Reuben Castle, the Young Hope for America'—not 'Reuben Castle, the Big Name in North Dakota.' On the other hand, there is a certain singularity in relating the candidacy to North Dakota. It gives a sense of the unity of the republic. You see what I mean, don't you, Susan?"

"Yes indeed. But the senator's attachment to his home state is pretty well recognized. After all, he was, for four years, North Dakota's sole representative in the House."

Reuben spoke up. "Hal, enough. I will announce from Washington."

"I was thinking you'd make that decision. Now, on when to do it. Let's go for next month, October. That puts us three months ahead of the Iowa caucuses. And it's a good time of year to pick up money. I've got *that* campaign planned. We'll want to shoot for $35 million to go through New Hampshire. If we win there, we'll go for the heavy stuff, and we'll get it. Susan, what've you got in the senator's schedule that we care about for October?"

"There's a trip to Israel, third week."

"Don't mess with that."

"And a few speeches. Miami, Notre Dame, Seattle. How about October 15?" She ticked the date and handed the calendar over to Reuben for approval. He stretched out his legs, leaned back on the sofa, and scrutinized the book.

"Sounds okay. I hope between now and then Saddam Hussein doesn't retire to a monastery, and the stock market doesn't go haywire-up."

"All right," Kaltenbach said, "October 15. Next item I've got to raise is Priscilla. I saw some complaints last winter about her...behavior...in Tallahassee."

Reuben froze. Then broke into a smile. "Oh, that's right—she talked about entering the contest for the Orange Bowl."

"The what?"

"The Orange Bowl."

Harold Kaltenbach was formal about all matters that touched on football. "Are you saying she thought the Orange Bowl was a beauty contest?"

"I think she gave a couple of people that impression."

Susan said nothing. She too was inclined to smile. But this would not be right, not with Harold Kaltenbach, All-American 1950. They had touched now the only other subject he took as seriously as presidential politics.

"The thing is," Kaltenbach said, looking Reuben straight in the eye, "we can't run the risk that she becomes a comic figure. She'll have to be front and center on October 15. But she'll obviously be okay at eleven A.M.—"

"Maybe we should announce at ten A.M.?"

Harold Kaltenbach frowned. He thought it right to remove jollity from *this* discussion. His voice was now even. *Deadly even*. Susan's amusement, set down in her special shorthand, was entirely private.

"We'll be setting up critical dates in New Hampshire and Iowa. Some will be breakfast meetings. She can go to those."

Reuben wondered whether he should tell Harold that Priscilla hadn't gotten up for breakfast in ten years. He decided against it. He'd just…put that problem off. Along with other problems.

CHAPTER 41

Winnipeg, Manitoba, September 1991

Henry Griswold knocked on the door of the hotel suite. He was bearded and imposing, gray-haired, formal in deportment.

Reuben quickly got down to business. It helped that the room was fusty Victorian. The curtains were full and ancient, the table was massive, and the sunlight was dimmed by the thick glass. Reuben cleared his throat. "Mr. Griswold, I wish that the business between us should remain entirely confidential. As you know, I am in politics, and have attained some prominence. For reasons I do not have to expand upon, what I am here to discuss with you is personal and is to remain personal. Is there any problem with that?"

"None whatever, Senator." Griswold's voice had just enough animation to denote to Reuben that he was not speaking to a stuffed dummy. Griswold bent his head just a degree or two. Middle-class Canadian deference—it crossed Reuben's mind— to a live United States senator.

"On the matter of fees, in this envelope you will find $5,000. That is a deposit on your consultancy. I will get to you anything in excess of that which I eventually owe you."

"How am I to be in touch with you?" In Griswold's hand a leather pad materialized, a gold pencil attached.

"You have my private telephone number. If you wish to send a letter by post, here is how to do it." He gave Jim Stannard's address. "Just put 'For Reuben' on the envelope."

Griswold nodded and pocketed the envelope Reuben handed him. "How shall I make out a receipt?"

"Don't bother. I don't feel I need to protect myself. At that level."

"So, what can I do for you, Senator?"

"Here is a summary of the relevant events. I was a student at the University of North Dakota in Grand Forks. In October 1969, I learned that my girlfriend was pregnant. We discussed various options but did not come to a conclusion. Then in November she asked me to drive with her to her hometown, which is the village of Letellier, south from here about—"

"I know the town. As a child my wife attended the convent school there."

That news was not happily greeted. Reuben was not in search of orthodoxy from his lawyer.

"It turned out that her destination was the rectory of the Catholic church there. She introduced me to the priest who had baptized her twenty-one years before."

"This priest, is he alive?"

"I don't know. He was already elderly in 1969. Anyway, after reminiscing with him for a few minutes, my lady—she is called, was called, Henrietta Leborcier"—he waited while Griswold wrote on his notepad—"told the priest that she wished him to proceed to marry us. I remember protesting, in some way or other, but she was very determined and most anxious that her child—"

"Your child?"

"Yes, our child—should at birth have both a mother and a father." He paused.

Griswold sat in his armchair, motionless.

"I simply have no memory of other details—I was pretty much overwhelmed by the whole thing. I do remember that we knelt for the priest's blessing after exchanging vows, and then there was the church ledger, which she signed, and I signed—I think. I must have."

"On your return to your university, did you discuss your marriage?"

"No. We agreed that we would not speak of it to *anybody*. My closest friend knew about the pregnancy, but not—or so at least I believe—about the marriage, or pseudo-marriage.

"Anyway, Henrietta and I agreed that she would, at the end of the term, leave for Paris, where her father was a university professor. I would proceed to graduation at Grand Forks."

"And then?"

"I came to my senses in the spring, and got word to her that I did not wish to continue our liaison."

"And the child?"

"I was penniless, Mr. Griswold. Her father had a university position and, I thought, savings."

"Did you ever hear from her again?"

"No. Not from that day to this."

"You proceeded with your life and your career?"

"Yes. I went to Vietnam as a soldier. I was discharged in 1972 and went to law school at the University of Illinois. I did not finish. I had come to the attention of the North Dakota Democratic Party, and I was quickly drawn into politics."

"You married?"

"Yes. In 1975. I was by then actively involved in politics, and the next year I was elected to Congress, as the sole member from North Dakota in the House of Representatives. North Dakota, like Wyoming and Montana and a couple of other states, gets two senators but only a single congressman.

"When I married, our wedding was amply noticed in the press, in part because I was already being spoken of as a congressional candidate, in part because my wife had been Miss America two years earlier."

"Who else knew of your liaison with Ms. Leborcier?"

"There were several classmates who knew us to be together a great deal at college. One of them, as I say, was an especially intimate friend. He and I are estranged, because he took offense at my breaking it off with...Henrietta. He is now a successful attorney in Grand Forks."

"Name?"

"Eric Monsanto."

"I know the name."

"But even he—on this I am not absolutely certain. We had been in the habit of sharing our secrets but I didn't want to tell even him of the marriage—alleged marriage."

"But he knew of the pregnancy?"

"Yes. It happened, so to speak, under his auspices. He and his girlfriend, and Henrietta and I, spent the night at his father's duck blind on Devil's Lake. And it was Monsanto who passed on the news to Henrietta that I had decided to end the...courtship. I have no reason to believe that she ever told him that—in her opinion—we had actually been married."

"You wish to know how that...marriage, or whatever one calls it, appears in Manitoba records?"

"Yes. Here is what, using my own resources, I have established. The church registry at Saint Anne's in Letellier records that on November 18 Henrietta and I were 'married.' "

Griswold made another note.

Reuben went on. "One point occurs to me, having to do with the civil authorities. I remember when I was *really* married, to Priscilla. We needed to apply for a marriage license a few days ahead of time. I certainly didn't do that with Henrietta. Surely any marriage performed by a priest without a valid marriage license from the Province of Manitoba would have been illegal, and therefore null?"

Griswold made a note: "So the first thing to find out is whether, at the Vital Statistics Agency in Winnipeg, there is any record of a marriage license having been issued, in November 1969, to... Leborcier and Castle."

"Yes."

Griswold looked up from his notepad. "If it does... if such a document exists... other than to advise you that it exists, what more would you seek, Senator?"

"Its destruction, Mr. Griswold."

Reuben had thought this out. Perhaps Griswold would simply leave the room.

But he didn't.

Bill Rode had done good work.

CHAPTER 42

Boulder, September 1991

The postcard from Justin had brought on dismemberment in her emotional life, Henrietta acknowledged late at night, after trying for hours to fall asleep. That postcard had collapsed her self-hypnosis. Her son now knew who his father was, his very public father. On divulging it all to Amy, Henrietta had finally acquired at least a counselor. She thought, self-reproachfully, of all those years devoted to keeping her father and her aunt—and her growing boy—ignorant of the true story. Her father had died never knowing that he had a son-in-law who was not dead in Vietnam, but very much alive in Washington.

Having turned now to Amy—motherly friend, professional superior, and warm companion—she felt all the more keenly the need for her company. Amy and Henri crossed paths many times a day in the great Chinook Library, where they both worked, but if Henri wanted uninterrupted time with Amy she needed to make special arrangements. Amy was always obliging. "We can have lunch, Henri, how's that? . . . You'd rather not? After work then? Maybe at your place—John won't be home till dinnertime. . . . So that's simple: we'll meet at your place. Is five-fifteen okay?"

Henri brought Amy a cup of the strong Colombian coffee she liked, and then gave her the letter from Jean-Paul to read.

In that letter Gallic indirectness was gone. Henri observed Amy struggling with the French and finally retrieved the letter from her. "Oh, Amy, let me translate. That first passage—Never mind. It just says how much he...loves me, and how...determined he is to 'open the door to our happiness.' He has been delayed returning from Paris, and he wants to stop off in Washington on his way here."

She leaned back in her chair and put the letter on her lap. Before she started reading, she said: "Amy, I don't know how much of this you already know, since you were friends with both JP and Stephanie. Anyway, JP is a close friend of a... apparently a very tenacious lawyer called—let me get it right"— she turned her eyes down to the letter—"Harrison Ledyard. Their wives were first cousins. JP and his wife—I never knew Stephanie, but I know you did—JP and Stephanie had the Ledyard daughter living with them in Paris for an entire year. It's that kind of family closeness."

Henri turned back to the letter and read slowly, giving it idiomatic translation: "I wish you to authorize me to retain the Ledyard...the firm of Ledyard...to pursue the matter of your marriage. 'La question de ton mariage.'...Any investigation will require your authorization. When dear Stephanie died, I inherited some money and can easily pay whatever costs pile up, which will not be large because Harrison is like my brother. Dear dear Henri, I wish you to send a telegram to Harrison Ledyard, saying—it must be in English of course—saying: 'This telegram authorizes the firm of Covington & Burling to represent me in matters which will be divulged to Harrison Ledyard by Professor Jean-Paul Lafayette.' The telegram must be there when I arrive in Washington on September 20." Henrietta put the letter to one side.

"Amy, I need advice. Legal, yes. But also moral. I need to know whether I am free to remarry. After twenty-one years' desertion. When I gave the impression that my husband was dead in Vietnam, obviously others thought I was free to re-marry. Only I—no one else—knew that the man I married was alive. I hid it from Justin, but now, in just a few days, he has come to know it all."

"Henri, have you—"

"And now I must decide— "

"Henri! *Stop talking for a minute!* Now. Answer my questions."

Henri bent her head, a lock of hair falling over her cheek. She left it there.

"My first question: have you heard anything from Justin about what he intends to do? He has some pretty hot informa-tion, at a time when Senator Castle is in the papers practically every day."

"No. I tried to phone him right after I got his card. He wasn't in, but I left a message asking him please to say nothing until we met and discussed the matter."

"Did he reply?"

"Yes. By postcard." She reached to her desk, a tense smile on her face.

She handed the postcard to Amy, who had no problem with the French on this one. It consisted of two words: "Maman, d'accord." But then pasted on one half of the card was a news photo of Senator Reuben Castle. Printed below it was the legend: "President, Bigamists for Castle."

Henri sniffled. But she finally capitulated, and smiled along with Amy.

And then she said, drying her tears with a tissue, "Before I met Jean-Paul, I never thought seriously about the question of annulment. I had always assumed that it was not possible. Obviously the marriage had been consummated. But now I've done some looking around in the library. The Vatican texts I found all agree that if one of the parties harbors an intention not to commit to a lifetime together, then the marriage never took place as a Christian union. It is therefore annullable. And Reuben couldn't have intended a lifetime together, given what he did just a few months later.

"On the legal question, I can't deny Jean-Paul permission to conduct an investigation. Of course, I know enough to ease the work of his friend Harrison Ledyard. What do you think of this text? I drafted it before I telephoned you." She passed the sheet of paper over.

TO HARRISON LEDYARD. THIS AUTHORIZES YOU TO PURSUE SUCH INQUIRIES AS WILL BE OUTLINED TO YOU BY JEAN-PAUL LAFAYETTE ON THE UNDERSTANDING THAT NO REVELATIONS WILL BE MADE ABOUT MY PERSONAL LIFE WITHOUT MY EXPRESS PERMISSION.

"I signed it, 'Henriette Leborcier Durban.' That, after all, is the name on my passport."

"You will telephone JP?"

"Yes. When he reaches Washington. That will be next Friday. I will tell him everything I know."

"Have you decided how to proceed?"

"Yes. I want very much to marry Jean-Paul."

"Well. If your fancy lawyer in Washington can't arrange for that, you'll just have to—"

"Get a fancier lawyer!"

They clasped each other's hands.

"Thanks, Amy. Thanks."

CHAPTER 43

Washington/Manhattan, September 1991

On Thursday, early in the afternoon, Susan rang Reuben on the intercom. "It's Jim Stannard. I know you want him put through when he calls."

"Yep." He pressed the lighted button.

"Reub, the guy you told me about in Canada has sent a special-delivery letter for you."

"You haven't opened it, Jim?"

"Of course not. But on the outside of the sealed envelope is a note. I'll read it to you: 'Sir: I think you will want to telephone me provided you receive this before two P.M. on September 26.' September 26 is today. The note goes on, 'In the envelope is material you will want on file. Yours, H. Griswold.' "

"Shoot me the telephone number."

"204-349-9221."

"Thanks. I'll send Susan for the envelope. Or maybe I'll pick it up myself. I've got a joint committee meeting at four."

"Okay. If I wake up and read you own the Brooklyn Bridge, I want in on it."

• • •

Reuben dialed the number, and Henry Griswold was on the line. "I have important information, Senator. But the reason I had you telephone is that I am going to be in New York on business tonight and all day tomorrow, Friday. You could meet me in New York tomorrow, or, on Saturday, I could travel down to Washington and meet with you there."

Reuben opened his appointment book. "Does New York, six P.M. tomorrow, sound okay?"

After a pause, "Yes. I expect to be back from the courthouse well before then."

"Where do we meet?"

"I suggest the offices of Taggart Brothers—156 West 56th Street. That's near Seventh Avenue."

"Ask for you by name?"

"No. Get off at the twenty-third floor, turn right, go into the Taggart offices. I'll be in room 2337."

He told Priscilla the next morning that he'd be away in New York on business later in the day, but might be back before bedtime.

"You mean *my* bedtime?"

"No, no way I could be back *that* early."

"So we can't have any fun until *Saturday*?"

"I'll manage to have some fun."

She sat up on the bed. "Don't you go havin' fun without me, Reuben. Senator Reuben."

He kissed her on the forehead and said he'd try to make it home "before all the fun is spent."

"Bring me somethin' from Tiffany's."

"Like a diamond bracelet?"

"Hmm. Yes. But don't forget to put your card in the box. Otherwise I might get it mixed up."

He poked her in the stomach with a finger, and blew her another kiss.

Walking up Seventh Avenue, Reuben found himself wishing he were less readily recognizable. He knew that relative invisibility was possible to achieve. Kaltenbach had told him that some public figures—even some movie stars—can go from one end of a city to the other without being stopped by a single person. "But then you'll run into the bit player in a movie or the guy who wrinkles his brow on TV to tell you about erectile dysfunction, and he might not make it three blocks without somebody recognizing him. Even if they think it was somebody else! You remember Adolphe Menjou?"

"Sort of," Reuben had said.

"Well, just about everybody who had a mustache and a sort of a dapper look, which means most barbers and all French barbers, was stopped because he was Adolphe Menjou, only usually he wasn't."

Reuben paused to extend his hand to a greeter carrying a Bergdorf-Goodman bag. "Thanks. Thanks a lot. I'll pass your word to the Senate!" *Don't slow your walking pace.* Maybe he should take to wearing a hat—hats often confuse people. Trouble with that is Jack Kennedy made wearing hats unconstitutional. At least for presidents. Or presidents-elect. Reuben wasn't that. Yet. Maybe he would buy a hat just for when he had to walk a few blocks in a city.

He returned the greeting of the black woman at the reception desk. "Thanks. Thanks very much, ma'am." In the elevator, no one addressed him. It helped, in discouraging impromptu interruptions, to appear engrossed in a newspaper. His *Washington Post*, held up in front of him, told of the FDA's quest for authority to regulate tobacco consumption. Thank God North Dakota isn't a tobacco-growing state!

He followed instructions and knocked on the door of 2337. Griswold was seated behind a desk. He rose, and pointed to the chair opposite.

"We've got a complicated situation in Letellier. And in Winnipeg. Let's deal with Winnipeg first.

"The Vital Statistics Agency records that a marriage license in your name and that of Henrietta Leborcier was issued on Wednesday, November 14, 1969."

"Does it say whether it was mailed or picked up?"

"Presumably mailed. The register says, 'Care Saint Anne's Church, 119 First Avenue, Letellier.' The document was in a loose-leaf binder. The page recording your license has been... withdrawn." Griswold handed a folder over to Reuben. "It can always be reinserted at the agency, should you choose to do that."

Reuben nodded. He slipped the folder into his briefcase. "And then?"

"And then I arranged to send someone to Letellier. My associate, Dumont, went to Saint Anne's and asked if he could examine the church records for November 1969. The pastor, Father Daniel, said there had recently been interest shown in his church records for that month. 'You are representing whom?' the priest

asked. Dumont said that he was tracking down Henrietta Leborcier because of a bequest.

"Father Daniel said the parish kept records of baptisms, first
communions, confirmations, marriages, and funerals, records
accessible to responsible parties. He took Dumont to his study
and pulled down a heavy leather-bound volume. Dumont examined it and looked for November 1969.

"And, yes, the names are there. The matrimony is recorded
on November 18, and there are the signatures of the two principals." Griswold paused.

"*I remember!*" Reuben thumped his forehead with his right
hand. "The marriage license!"

"You remember what, Senator?"

"We didn't *have* a marriage license!"

"Then how is it that you were listed in the registry as having
married?"

"What happened," Reuben spoke now excitedly, "was that
when Henri—Henrietta—proposed that we should be married,
the father asked, did we have a marriage license? Of course we
didn't. But dear old Father Lully, dumb shit, said, 'Never mind.
I have marriage-license application forms. Just fill one out, and
I'll send it on to Winnipeg. On account of the required twenty-
four-hour waiting period...' I remember exactly! He was count-
ing out the days on his fingers—he said, 'They'll get the
application day after tomorrow, November 13, send the license
back to me the next day, November 14. To play it safe, I'll set the
wedding date at November 18.' That is exactly what happened."

"That corresponds with our examination," Griswold nodded. "The Vital Statistics Agency reports that the Castle-

Leborcier license was issued on November 14. And the church registry records the marriage on November 18." Griswold raised his hand. "Is there any way you could prove that you were in Grand Forks on November 18?"

"I doubt it. That's one week after the actual date, meaning that it was also a Sunday. We—*I*, actually; I was chairman of the Student Council—I got to use the university station wagon on Sundays. That's how we drove to Letellier. But the offices of the *Dakota Student*—I was also the editor of the student newspaper—are closed on Sundays, so I wouldn't have been on record as being there. And there are no classes Sundays—and in any case professors don't keep rosters of class attendance."

"Senator—" Griswold had raised his hand again as if to arrest the flow of reminiscences. "Senator, it doesn't look to me as if you can prove that you and...Ms. Leborcier...weren't in Letellier on the day recorded in the registry of Saint Anne's. But"—he needed to shake his raised hand to stop Reuben—"I'm not sure it would make any difference."

"What do you mean? If the church records are just plain *false?*"

"If they are false, the Province of Manitoba could charge Father Lully with a clerical misdemeanor—if he's still alive. But your signatures are in the parish registry. So the good father acted impulsively? What kind of punishment would you expect would be meted out? For writing 'Sunday, November 18' instead of 'Sunday, November 11'—twenty years ago? As long as that registry survives, there is no way you can guard against the charge that you were married to Henrietta Leborcier in Letellier on November 18, 1969."

• • •

Bill and Susan were waiting for him at the airport. Susan handed him the large manila envelope. "This is what you asked for." He nodded, and she said, "See you Monday, Senator," and left.

Bill drove Reuben to the restaurant on G Street. They were shown to a booth in a dimly lit corner. They ordered drinks and steaks.

Rode was quiet. He knew something was up. He waited for Senator Castle to set his own pace.

Castle spoke randomly about duties ahead and projects undertaken and the need to be present for Monday's vote on the tobacco bill.

The steaks were served, and Reuben started cutting into his, but without paying it the kind of appreciative attention he habitually showed when served good steak. He filled his wineglass.

"Can I trust you, Bill?"

"Senator—Reuben—I will do anything for you. Anything at all."

"You realize I'm going to be president of the United States."

"Yes, sir. I know that. That's where you belong. And anything I can do to make that happen, I'm doing for the benefit of my country."

Reuben took out Griswold's card from his pocket and handed it to Bill. On the back were written a name and a telephone number.

"This man," he pointed to the card, "knows what to do. What *you* have to do is go to Winnipeg, check in at the Radisson

Downtown, and call and let him know where you are. When he arrives at your hotel room, hand him this envelope. That's all. Just make sure it's him."

"How do I know it's him?"

"He's been told to show you his passport. His name is René Benoît. Give him the envelope and get back to Washington."

"Consider it done, Reuben."

CHAPTER 44

Letellier, October 1991

Emile Chevalier stared at the embers. His three colleagues rested, one of them flat on his back on the wet grass. A second one stood, leaning on the fire-hose carriage. "Okay to roll it back up, Chief?"

"I guess so. The fire's certainly out. There's nothing left to hose down."

Indeed there wasn't *anything* left at 119 First Avenue for fire to consume.

Chevalier angled his powerful flashlight to the right, then scanned left, moving his hand slowly, directing the beam searchingly.

Plainly visible was the limned outline of what had been the porch. And there was the phenomenon of the surviving brick chimney—this had tantalized Emile as a boy and, later, vexed him. He first remarked the surviving chimney as a fifteen-year-old, permitted for the first time to serve as assistant to his daredevil father, fire chief of Letellier. What he noticed was that chimneys, in some shape, survive even heat and flames that would treat solid steel safes as if they were made of wax. The chimney would somehow stay up, often for days, even weeks, after the fire was out.

Chevalier was satisfied by the performance of the Letellier Fire Squadron, if not exactly proud. They had God to thank for Claudette's having reached the telephone downstairs before the fumes overcame her. This would have happened to her even five or six minutes later. But it was too late for poor Father Daniel, asleep in his bedroom on the second floor.

It was reasonably assumed that he hadn't suffered. His charred corpse was lying on what remained of his bed as if he had never wakened. His pipe was at his side. Emile would arrive at no judgment on that delicate score: every year, at the harvest fair, he touched down on the danger of smoking in bed.

What else could it have been? It was just the beginning of October, and there was no sign that a fire had recently been lit in any of the rectory's three fireplaces. Yet it would be unusual for a spark from a tobacco pipe to set off that sort of class-A fire—a fire that had consumed so quickly, even hungrily, the substantial wood-frame house. It was mysterious. He'd say that to the fire examiner from Winnipeg. He simply declined to rule that the fire was accidental.

The inspector would be on the scene before noon. Chief Chevalier had already reported the fire over the phone, describing, in the professional shorthand expected, its deadly consequences.

Emile very much needed to sleep; so did the three other members of the fire company. There was only the one formal job left to do, and his camera was ready to take sequential photos, going right around the 800-square-foot carcass of the old rectory. That would be done well before the sun came up. He would look especially hard for clues.

CHAPTER 45

South Bend, October 1991

Justin liked to tease Allard about golf, a sport Allard had pursued two or three times a week ever since they began life together at Notre Dame. When on Thursday, lugging his clubs, Allard huffed his way into their room late in the afternoon, Justin leaned back in his desk chair and, speaking in French as was their custom, said, "Allard, I had a call from the dean's office. Canada has instituted a draft and you are to report to Quebec for duty." The jape had a lifetime of almost two seconds, which Justin thought justified the effort. He went back to work while Allard pulled a towel from the closet and strode off to the showers.

But Allard was a good sport, and an hour later he leaned over from his desk on the other side of their shared room and removed the headphone from his ears. He was listening, as he regularly did, to the Canadian Broadcasting station in Montreal. Justin broke in: "What's hot in Canada, Allard?"

"Tais-toi," Allard half whispered. "Your mother's town in Manitoba is Letellier, right?"

Justin nodded, and Allard adjusted the knob. The broadcaster in Montreal was giving the nightly news, province by province. In Manitoba, he reported, a fire in the town of Letellier had demolished the rectory of the Catholic church, leaving the pastor, who was asleep when the fire started, dead. Allard turned up the sound. "The deceased is Father Henry Daniel, a native of Ottawa, who was for many years the pastor of Saint Anne's, the adjacent church, known for its modern crystal-glass cross, which was destroyed. Mademoiselle Claudette Crognard, the housekeeper at the rectory, survived but is receiving treatment at the hospital in nearby Altona. The Winnipeg fire examiner has reported that the cause of the devastating fire was not immediately apparent, and that investigation continues.

"In Alberta—"

Justin signaled Allard to turn the radio down. "Saint Anne's," he said, "was my mother's parish. She was baptized in that church."

"Well, I'm sorry, Justin. I don't guess there's anything the government of Canada can do for you." Allard was not being sarcastic. As the son of the Canadian ambassador, he liked to accumulate Canadian information of interest, usually on matters such as student scholarships and travel. If there was any chance he could intercede for an American friend on official business he was always willing to try.

"Allard..." Justin hesitated for a minute—but what was there to lose? "Allard, it happens that my mother was married in that rectory and that the record of that marriage was kept there, with other official records."

"Again, Justin, I'm sorry. But there are other records, surely, of that marriage."

"It's a mysterious situation. Let me think about it for a bit."

After a few minutes' silence he picked up the telephone and put in a call to Maria Cervantes at the university in Grand Forks.

When he had finished speaking with her he said to Allard: "There *is* something you might be able to do for me. The only other record of the marriage would be in Winnipeg, at what they call the Vital Statistics Agency. Allard, could you arrange for someone there to look for records of a marriage license?"

"Certainement," he said. "Write down the names."

At noon the next day Justin found a note on his desk. It was from Allard, reporting that no record of a marriage license in 1969 or 1970 for the two people named was to be found at the Vital Statistics Agency.

Justin sat at his desk. His frustration raged.

Again he picked up the phone and reached Dean Cervantes. She had an answer to the question he had put to her yesterday: nothing had survived the rectory fire.

Justin walked, with some deliberation, to the offices of *The Observer*. Student reporters and editors were hard at work on the large issue scheduled for homecoming week. Harry Jenks, a senior editor, was in charge.

Justin greeted his colleagues and sat down at a computer in the editors' room. He pulled the file from his briefcase and began to write.

"Senator Reuben Castle, who will appear on campus on October 28, is expected to run for president. 'The coast is pretty clear,' to quote Professor Chafee of the Government Department.

"The president of the Lecture Series Committee, which is sponsoring the visit by Senator Castle, goes further than that. 'He is still a long shot,' says Henry Fisher '92, 'but there is genuine enthusiasm for him and I think his visit to South Bend will confirm this.' "

Justin gave the particulars of the forthcoming visit and went on. "Senator Castle is a special favorite of the Democratic Party's liberal wing. He identified himself with it as an undergraduate activist at the University of North Dakota, campaigning vigorously to end the Vietnam War.

"Mr. Castle served in Vietnam and entered the law school at the University of Illinois in 1972, but left it after one year in order to begin an active career in politics. In 1976 he was elected to Congress, as the sole representative of North Dakota, and four years later was elected to the Senate, succeeding Republican Senator Milton R. Young, who was retiring."

Justin drew a deep breath and plunged in.

"A visitor to Grand Forks, looking into student life at the University of North Dakota in the late 1960s, would find evidence of Reuben Castle almost everywhere. He was the editor in chief of the *Dakota Student*, the undergraduate newspaper, and he was chairman of the Student Council.

"There is speculation, in Grand Forks, that as an undergraduate he impregnated a fellow student, whom he proceeded to marry at a secret ceremony in Letellier, a town in the Canadian province of Manitoba seventy miles north of Grand Forks.

"Senator Castle has never acknowledged that marriage—" He stopped.

He shut down the computer. Then he restarted it and printed out what he had written. He grabbed the pages from the printer and stuffed them into his satchel. He jotted a note to Jenks. "Harry, sorry I didn't get the story on Castle finished, but I won't miss the deadline."

Back at his room in Dillon Hall he found a note from Student Affairs taped to the door. "For Justin Durban: Please call Mr. Eric Monsanto at 701-777-2020."

Justin picked up the telephone and dialed the Monsanto office, but at that moment Allard came into the room. Justin put the receiver down to abort the call. He didn't want even Allard, by now his closest friend, to hear what he was going to say.

Allard was back from class and preparing to go to the links. He was lively on the matter of the missing marriage license. "That kind of thing doesn't happen in Winnipeg. I don't mean people don't steal things, but it's unusual enough to make you feel that somebody was up to something. When you add that to the rectory being destroyed, you get a smelly situation." He reached for his golf cap and then his clubs. "Don't suppose you want to take up the sport—sport?"

Justin smiled and waved his roommate out the door.

Quickly he dialed again. When he heard Eric Monsanto's voice, he said, "Mr. Monsanto, before you tell me what you have on your mind, I'm sorry about that deception when I was up with you a few weeks ago. I've been on a—well, a hot story, and I had to keep a low profile."

"Look, Justin. I know who you are. I tracked you down, which wasn't hard. I did the positive-ID bit—there aren't many

Notre Dame students born in Paris. But I didn't really need to do that."

"What do you mean, sir?"

"I mean that before I found out that Justin Durban was born in Paris in May 1970 to Henrietta Leborcier Durban, I knew who you were. Maybe you've never seen a picture of your father when he was twenty-one years old."

"I see what you mean, sir. Yes, my mother...has a picture like that, but she doesn't show it around."

"I'm calling you about the fire in the church in Letellier."

"I heard about it—my roommate listens to Canadian radio."

"Did you know that the priest was killed, in his bedroom in the rectory?"

Justin's voice was unsteady. "Yes, the radio report did say that Father Daniel had been killed."

"You knew him?"

"I went there. The day after I met you. I talked with him. He let me look at the church records. That's how I found out about my father."

"Found out what?"

"That he was married there to my mother. On November 18, 1969. How—I mean, what was it that killed Father Daniel?"

"Smoke. The Winnipeg fire examiner has been looking at the scene for two days now. He suspects foul play."

"But why?" Justin's mind clicked onto the inquiry Allard had made. "Mr. Monsanto, here's something maybe you should know."

"I'm listening."

"My roommate here is the son of the Canadian ambassador to the United States. He knows like *everybody*. I asked him to check in Winnipeg, at the Vital Statistics Agency, to see if there was a marriage license on file for my mother. And my father." He would need to get used to referring to his father.

"Did they come up with anything?"

"No. That's my point. There was no record of the marriage, Castle-Leborcier."

"So that means there's now no record of the marriage. In Letellier. In Winnipeg. In Canada, I guess."

"Sir. Did you know they had been...married?"

Eric paused. "I guessed it. Actually, it was more than just a guess. It was the way they behaved when the three of us were together. And there were references to Saint Anne's. And to, like, 'the great day at Saint Anne's.' When I wrote to your mother in Paris I never put it to her that she was married, but everything I said was—as if they were married."

"So what's to be done, sir?"

"You can call me Eric. What's to be done is for me to get in touch with the Winnipeg people. Tell them about the missing documents. See if they have anything going on in the investigation in Letellier. Is there a phone number where I can reach you directly?"

"Yes. It's 574-631-2811. Meanwhile, I'm trying to think whether to call Maman and tell her about the fire. We haven't spoken since I was at Saint Anne's and saw the church register. But she knows that I know. I sent her a postcard from Letellier. I guess this was a different priest from the one that married her. Baptized her, too."

"Yes. Father Daniel had only been at Saint Anne's for about eight years. I'll call you when I have some information."

"Thank you."

CHAPTER 46

South Bend, October 1991

On Monday Allard told Justin, just returned from his nine o'clock class, that he had had a call from his father. *Le grand ambassadeur!*

"Anything wrong?"

"Not that I know of. But I am to report to a law office in South Bend—I have the name written down. Papa said there was some international formality involved. I hope I haven't sponsored a visa for a Canadian who is engaged in serial murder."

The roommates met for lunch.

"Ecoute! That is some bird running the RCMP office in Winnipeg."

"What did he want with you?" Justin asked.

"He wants you now more than he wants me." Allard passed Justin a card.

AUGUST BELCOURT
ROYAL CANADIAN MOUNTED POLICE

The card included address and telephone number. "He is one tough hombre. What it comes down to is your dad's—Senator Castle's—business, the wedding and the papers. Belcourt came to see me because I was the guy—they tracked it back—who called Vital Statistics and asked someone to look for the marriage license. They put that together with the fire and the dead priest. Leborcier-Castle is now a very hot number with the RCMP."

After lunch Justin went to the same South Bend law office and reported to the tall man with the stiff gray crew cut.

Commander Belcourt came quickly to the point. "We are calculating that the church was burned down by an arsonist and that his motive was to destroy records involving your mother—and, well, Senator Reuben Castle.

"This is not the time or the place to explore the relationship between him and your mother. We're interested only in finding the arsonist and the person who commissioned him." He looked down at his notes. "You visited the church, we have down here, on September 4. After visiting with"—again he consulted his notes—"Mr. Eric Monsanto in Grand Forks, North Dakota. Mr. Monsanto is known to the lieutenant governor. They have worked together. We have been in touch with him. We are interested in your visits and your purposes. You spoke with Father Daniel, the victim?"

"Yes. Yes, sir."

"And do you remember the housekeeper? Claudette Crognard?"

"I do indeed. She was kind enough to give me some cookies and an apple."

"You found what you were looking for?"

"Yes."

"Describe what you were looking for."

"I was looking for evidence that my—that Henrietta Leborcier had married Reuben Castle. There was evidence of this in the register, in an entry dated November 18, 1969."

Justin did not tell Commander Belcourt that he had photographed the page of the parish register. Perhaps this was something better held back for the moment.

"Were there signatures of the principals?"

"Yes, sir."

"Did you recognize the handwriting?"

"I recognized the handwriting of my mother. I am not familiar with the handwriting of . . . my father."

The commander was called to the telephone. He returned and sat down with a special assurance.

"We have the arsonist. We shall deal with him."

CHAPTER 47

South Bend, October 1991

Justin had had no further meetings with Professor Lejeune since the one in May. When he returned to South Bend in September, the French-department secretary gave him a curriculum, a class schedule (eight A.M., Monday through Friday), student names, and classroom assigned. Justin reported periodically on his students' progress, filing their grades. There was the one problem. Late in September, Justin had to notify the department that one of his students, Lawrence Abraham Custer, Class of '93, had failed every quiz so far. That development earned Assistant in Instruction Durban an ostensibly extemporaneous encounter with the captain of the football team, a magnificence named Ned Rodzinski. The two students were filing, in separate columns, into the dining hall. Captain Ned crossed over to Justin, nodded, and introduced himself. This was an act of ingratiation: the captain of the football team at Notre Dame did not need to identify himself to any living creature in South Bend.

"You know, Durban, Larry Custer is one of the best linemen on the team. Next year he could—I mean it's possible, he's that good—could be elected captain."

Justin said he hadn't known this.

"Maybe you didn't know that an athlete who is failing a course at midterm is forbidden to engage in any extracurricular activity."

Justin thought swiftly. One part of quick thinking, in a bind like this, is to know when disingenuous naïveté is appropriate. "Well, Ned, let's just hope he pulls his socks up before the midterm exam. I'm sure he will."

Ned smiled and rejoined his classmate Barbara, who was a cheerleader for Ned, on the field and off it.

It was late one afternoon soon after the Notre Dame–Michigan game that Justin had the call from the French-department secretary. Professor Lejeune wished to see him.

Justin worried that evening and the next morning. The football crisis having passed—it was two weeks until the midterm, and Custer had indeed pulled his socks up—he couldn't think of any problems with his teaching of French 10ab. His students were doing well, and he gave them two hours every week of office hours, during which he would help any student who came to see him.

Merde alors! If his commission as assistant in instruction was to be terminated, that would be because older teachers were now available, or student enrollment for the next semester was expected to diminish.

Lejeune addressed him in French: "Sit down; read this." Lejeune handed him a typed essay, a dozen pages long.

Justin put on his glasses and recognized, after half a page, the essay on Mallarmé that Allard had given him to read the week before.

"I've already read this, sir."

"You are familiar with it?"

"Well, yes. It was written by Allard de Minveille. He is my roommate. He gave it to me to read."

"Did you contribute to the writing?"

"No. Well, I told him I thought two or three paragraphs were unclear."

"Please find the paragraphs to which you were referring."

Justin went back to the paper, and began to read it page by page. In a few minutes he said, "He must have reworked it. It was where he wrote about the reception given to the early work of Mallarmé. But it seems clear to me now."

"Are you familiar with the biography of Mallarmé by Philippe Ducoquet?"

"No, sir."

"Minveille did not call this book to your attention?"

"No, sir."

Professor Lejeune leaned back in his chair. He looked at Justin and extended his hand for the paper. Justin returned it to him.

"I am responsible for the honor of the students who take my courses."

Justin nodded apprehensively.

Nothing more was said by Lejeune. He signaled the end of the meeting by picking up another manuscript. "Bien. Merci, Durban."

Justin got up, nodded, and went to the door.

Back in his room he sat down at his desk. He looked over at Allard's corner, on the other side of the room. His eyes went to the bookcase. Allard would not be back from the golf course for at least an hour.

He pondered the rows of books, perhaps 200 of them. He made up his mind, got up, and went over to the bookcase, scanning the titles. At the end of the second row, he saw the book he was looking for.

He took it down and leafed through the pages. The book was well marked by pencil lines and an occasional note in the margin, the handwriting discernibly Allard's. He came to the passage Professor Lejeune had called to his attention. It was underlined, perhaps fifty words.

Justin considered reckless action. Should he just remove the book? Destroy it?

What would that prove? He replaced the book, and a while later greeted a cheerful Allard back from the links, his golf cap stamped, NOTRE DAME 1992.

Allard put down his clubs and went to the little refrigerator, reaching for a Coke. "Tu désires?"

"No thanks."

"What did the Professor of Aloofness want with you?"

"He wanted to know if I had read your essay."

"The Mallarmé?"

"Yes."

Allard sat down at his desk. He lowered his head. "So he spotted the plagiarism. Son of a bitch!" He managed a laugh. "Did he think maybe *you* had written it?"

Justin said nothing. He picked up his satchel and went to the door. "I'm going to the library." He paused. "I hope you're still at Notre Dame when I get back. Why are some bright people so stupid?" That sounded especially scathing in French.

CHAPTER 48

Washington, October 1991

"Honey?"

"Yes?"

"Why do you say jus'... 'yes'?"

"Yes, *dear.*"

"You didn' use to be that way. Is it because I'm not Miss America any more?"

"Oh, Priscilla. You were a terrific Miss America. But that was 1973. You're not *supposed* to be Miss America for the rest of your life."

"You use to tell me I'd be *your* Miss America for *always.*"

Reuben was trying to read the draft of a speech. "*Always,* honey, came—and went."

"I'm thinkin' of goin' back to Dr. Ellsworth."

"Come on! He did your face just— "

"It was 1988."

"Well, you're not supposed to have your face done every three years."

"Marilyn Monroe did, I read."

"Well, dear Priscilla, you're not Marilyn Monroe."

She got up, walking with measured steps over to the stand-up mirror on the other side of the room. Easing her negligee

WILLIAM F. BUCKLEY JR.

over her shoulders, she bared her breasts. "Anythin' wrong with these?"

He looked up. He *knew* that would be a mistake, but it was done, and his staff was now at full, ineluctable attention. His voice took on the habitual hoarseness. "You wanting a little loving?"

She smiled and let her negligee fall to the floor.

Ten minutes later he rose, breathing hard. "I'm going to get myself something to drink."

"Well, put your shorts back on."

"Why? I like them off. Even if I don't have to go—like you— and look at myself in the mirror." But he did turn his head to the mirror, and stole a pleased glance at himself.

"Honey," her voice was silky, "since you're goin' downstairs, do something for your lovah?"

"Like what?" But of course he knew what she wanted from downstairs. "Okay, I'll bring it up."

At the bar, he measured the rum carefully, wondering if he could get away with giving her just two jiggers....No. There would be the quarreling, and to quiet that, he'd have to go back to the bar and get her another slug.

He brought up the rum and Coke, and for himself a cold beer.

She took a good gulp. "Honey, you know, I heard from three different people jus' in the last coupla days you're gonna be president. Not you're gonna *run* for president, you're gonna *be* president."

"Priscilla, I told you before, we just don't *talk* about that subject."

"Well, you're gonna *have* to 'talk about that subject,' like you put it, when you begin to, well, campaign for president. Bess said to me—you know Bess, she does my hair—she said you were gonna, well . . . go public next week."

Reuben was surprised. "Where'd she pick that rumor up?"

"I don' know. But she tol' me if I gave her the exact date, she'd fix me up to look real good."

"You look great, dear. Just great. But don't go and encourage rumors. If it's going to happen it's going to happen. —I'd better sleep in the study tonight. I have to be up real early."

"Well, don't wake *me* up real early, honey, 'less you want a little more poontang!"

He leaned over and kissed her.

In his study he looked at his watch. It wasn't yet midnight, and Susan worked late. But then Susan wouldn't mind if Reuben Castle rang her at three in the morning. He dialed her number. "My wife's hairdresser told her, like it was a scheduled thing, that we were ready to announce."

"Well, Reuben, maybe that's because you just about *are* ready to announce. You had it down for October 15—next Tuesday. Well, Hal just told me today to move it up by one day, so it will be on Monday. And *60 Minutes* is going to do you Sunday night. That'll tie in perfectly."

"I knew *60 Minutes* was cooking up something. They've been all over the place." He corrected himself silently. Not *quite* all

WILLIAM F. BUCKLEY JR.

over the place—*60 Minutes* hadn't poked around in Letellier, as far as he knew.

"You know, the Secret Service will put a detail on you beginning when you announce. Beginning Monday."

"I'll be working on my announcement tomorrow. We mustn't let Mike Wallace down."

"Oh, dear no, Reuben. We would *never* survive that."

"*Never!*" Reuben got into the act, exaggerating in his voice the unthinkability of letting Mike Wallace down.

CHAPTER 49

Manhattan, October 1991

"This guy *what*? Wants to see me about the Sunday program? About *tonight's* program?"

Don Hewitt never used more words than were needed to produce his documentaries exactly as he wished them seen. He was fiercely proud of meeting deadlines imposed by himself on himself, and proud of *60 Minutes'* record of dramatizing a subject or a news event in what seemed, to rival producers, a matter of, well, sixty minutes.

He would spend weeks and months on a segment, inching it along toward a completion not always visualized until the last minute. A dozen proposals rested, unfinished, in the can, pending news developments—turns in the fortunes of presidents and kings, bankers and poets, tennis stars and guitarists. Hewitt would air them when he thought the time was right.

He had considered doing Castle ever since the celebrated "debate" with General Westmoreland, and there was stray material in the can. But it wasn't until Friday, October 11, that Kaltenbach flat-out tipped him off—told him exactly when Castle would announce.

Hal Kaltenbach would never deceive Don Hewitt. Never did, never—Hewitt felt—would. People of true consequence on the American scene knew the long reach of *60 Minutes*, and Harold Kaltenbach was planning, no less, to make a young senator from North Dakota—*North Dakota!*—president of the United States. Hewitt sensed there might be something to it, this fielding of Reuben Castle for president. Kaltenbach, he knew very well, didn't dissipate his unique resources on out-of-sight long shots. So Hewitt made the deal: *60 Minutes* would go with it on Sunday. But in return, Castle had to announce his candidacy not on Tuesday, but on Monday, giving *60 Minutes* a fabulous scoop. Monday—tomorrow!

Hewitt had needed to prepare a memorable portrait-style segment in just two days. Mike Wallace, the senior broadcaster on *60 Minutes*, was alerted to go with it. He put his top researchers to work with his associate producer, Allan Stoops. It was past midnight Saturday when the phone rang—the special phone with the closely guarded number—and Stoops reported to Hewitt that the segment was completed. And that it was very good.

Now—three o'clock on Sunday afternoon—Stoops called again. "You know, Don, I've got a real feel for the work we did on Senator Castle. I think it's a great segment. But I'm telling you, you've got to see this kid—hear what he says, and see his face. This is what I call life and death." So Justin Durban was admitted to the apartment house on East 57th Street, only a few blocks crosstown from the studio.

A half hour later Hewitt had everyone assembled at the studio. Two writers, four cameramen, two editors, one makeup woman, three researchers. If Allan Stoops had been able to do so, he would have mobilized the Seventh Army to quarantine the building. No one was allowed in; no one was allowed out. A single telephone line, on Hewitt's desk, was operating. Twenty other lines were blocked.

And all Hewitt had to work with was a photograph of the senator as a twenty-year-old. Just that, and one live twenty-one-year-old. Calls to the young man's mother failed to reach her. But the Grand Forks lawyer was tracked down on the golf course. The RCMP commander was roused at home, as was the fire chief in Letellier. Showtime minus ten minutes, and Hewitt had three alternatives. The first was to show the original profile exactly as it had been prepared. The second was to kill it and run something from the can. The third was to run the revised segment.

Oh, God, the risks.

CHAPTER 50

Washington, October 1991

The house on M Street was full, and of course Priscilla had been right; the evening had to be organized by caterers. "There's no way Nellie and I can take care of fifty, sixty people—"

"Twenty or thirty people."

"—even if we gave them nothin' but popcorn. Reuben, think of just the *drinks*!"

"I thought we could get Dover to serve the drinks. He's done that for us before."

"So he does drinks. You got in mind offering *anything anybody* wants? Like mint juleps? Reuben, you should have had *60 Minutes* provide for this party. They're responsible, aren't they?"

He was now exasperated. "Look, Priscilla, they're going to feature *me* Sunday night, and they're going to say that *I'm* running for president and that *I'm* going to declare my candidacy the next day. But it's *my* candidacy that makes the news, not the fact that *they* are featuring it on *60 Minutes*."

"Well, you go and tell that to the people comin' here to see the *60 Minutes* show—why doesn' that make it a *60 Minutes* night?"

"Never mind." He shuddered at the thought of such logical

quagmires every week, once the campaign got under way, for...
October–December 1991, eleven weeks; January–November
1992, forty-three weeks.

Fifty-four weeks. Shee-yit.

Meanwhile there was Sunday night to worry about. Hell.
Okay. Let the caterers—after all, there were four of them—
figure out a way of handling all that. Keeping two dozen people
well hosed for a couple of hours...not an impossible assignment
for skilled Georgetown caterers.

Reuben was pleased by the reaction he got on Sunday afternoon
from Susan Oakeshott and Bill Rode. He had brought them together, most confidentially, to give them a preview of what he
proposed to say at eleven A.M. the next day at his press conference.

He tried the script out on them in a pretty dramatic way. He
stood—doors locked—at one end of Room 220 of the Senate
Office Building, which was where he would be making the announcement tomorrow. The room, frequently used for important political events, was permanently wired for television
cameras. There was provision for five cameras, and for as many
print reporters as turned up. Some of the guests who would be
coming to the house to watch 60 Minutes tonight would also be
there tomorrow. But they would not have heard this preview of
his announcement. Just Susan and Bill.

His tryout was designed as a dress rehearsal. No interruptions. Bill read out the exact text of the introduction that would
be given tomorrow by North Dakota's senior senator. Then Reuben spoke, and they clocked him at twenty-one minutes.

Not bad, he smiled. Not bad, considering that he had given advice on domestic policy *and* foreign policy, especially Iraq. He would inform the assembly that he planned to visit Israel the following week: "I think that any American official who plans to have a voice in foreign-policy decisions owes it to himself—and to the United States, and to the whole civilized world—to visit personally the Holy Land and try to understand what the people of Israel have done to preserve their ancient homeland."

In a copy of the text, Susan marked the passages at which Reuben could expect applause. There were eight such. Susan suggested a minor change in the formulation of Reuben's criticism of President Bush on the Iraq question. Reuben digested it, made the change, and then gave the corrected speech to Bill, who would have copies ready for distribution to the press at ten-thirty tomorrow, the big day.

There were twenty-six people at the modest house in Georgetown. They had begun arriving at six, and their mood was exuberant.

"This is a historic moment," Linda Bridgehouse said. "And a fine scoop for Mike Wallace." She smiled weightily.

Everyone had a chair and a drink by the time the famous tick-tick began. Then, to the universal dismay of the company, the screen went back to an unfinished football game. The screen indicated the time left to play in the fourth quarter: 2:12. "Oh, God!" Priscilla said. "They still have two hours and twelve minutes left to play."

"No," Reuben snapped at her. "It's two *minutes* twelve *sec-*

onds." He was visibly embarrassed by Priscilla's ignorance and then by his own impatience. "But with time-outs added to the minutes of play that could mean a delay of ten or fifteen minutes," he acknowledged. "So," he looked around, "everybody! Have another drink!"

"And another hot dog," Priscilla said. This brought on a round of applause, because little hot dogs indeed had been served, the buns nicely warmed, the mustard Dijon, the coleslaw fresh and spicy.

A quarter of an hour later, the evening's *60 Minutes* line-up was announced. There would be a segment on Joe Montana, who might be the greatest football player ever. Then an exposé on the drug company that produced Lipitor. Then the segment on Reuben Castle.

The third segment, when its turn finally came, was heralded by a head-on shot of the senator. There was august silence in the room. The screen showed Senator Castle in a half dozen situations—speaking, presiding over a committee meeting, substituting for General Westmoreland, at home in Georgetown—two-second spots.

"Tomorrow, *60 Minutes* has learned"—Mike Wallace's assured voice was even, but he managed a hint of drama—"Senator Reuben Castle will announce his candidacy for president of the United States. But there are certain things in his past which he won't be talking about."

On-screen, without identification, was a still picture of a young man looking down at a recent newspaper shot of Senator Castle. The camera turned then to a photo of a second young man. Mike Wallace said, "This was Reuben Castle when he was twenty years old."

Reuben froze in his chair.

There was no way to stop the irreversible footage, the irreversible story.

At the end of the segment there was silence. Bill Rode reached to turn the television off.

The guests filed silently, most of them, out the door. Some attempted a word or two with a cheerful edge. Reuben stood by with Priscilla, shaking hands. But after a minute or two he slid back from the doorway, leaving it to Priscilla to say good night, and good-bye.

In the kitchen, Reuben stretched to the telephone box and disconnected the two lines.

Susan arrived just after ten, by taxi. She kept her finger on the doorbell.

Priscilla finally peered through the venetian blind, and opened the door.

"Where is he?"

Priscilla pointed upstairs.

Reuben was seated in his study, watching the television news.

He turned the sound down. "What are you here to tell me, Susan?"

"What I guess you expected. We should call off the announcement tomorrow."

He nodded. "You heard from Kaltenbach?"

"Yeah. Nice twenty seconds on the phone. He said, 'Tell Reuben don't call me, I'll call him.' "

"You want a drink?"

"No."

Neither of them spoke. The sound was off, but pictures were being screened of Senator Reuben Castle and of the young man. Susan could discern that there were cameras outside an apartment house; the caption said it was in Boulder, Colorado, "the home of the first Mrs. Castle."

They both looked at the screen, and imagined the words being spoken.

"Okay, Susan. Call the announcement off."

She rose. "Good night, Senator."

He nodded. "Good night."

BOOK FOUR

CHAPTER 51

Manhattan/Devil's Lake, North Dakota, October 1991

Justin went from the studio to the Barclay Hotel, where CBS had gotten him a room. He had in hand an open plane ticket. In his room, after gulping down a steak dinner brought to him by room service, he opened it and stared down. "FROM: NYC." On the next line, "To: _____."

"You go ahead, fill in the destination you want," Mr. Wilson had told him, when Justin was ready to leave the studio. "Feel like going to Hawaii?"

Justin said nothing. He smiled, pocketing the ticket and the accompanying envelope. Written on it, in pencil, was "J. Durban. Reimbursed expenses, 60 Minutes, 10/13/91."

He turned the television set to channel 2 and fretted on seeing that the football game would probably bump into the sacred seven P.M. slot for *60 Minutes*. It did. It was fifteen minutes past the hour when the *60 Minutes* signal came on.

The broadcasters announced a segment on the great quarterback, a second segment on a drug sensation. And then—he stared at his father's face on the television screen. The segment he cared so much about was third in line. He looked at his watch. That meant it would come on just before eight o'clock. Well, he would be there.

He felt a renewal of the pounding heartbeat he had felt that afternoon when he was being interviewed and filmed. But finally it came on, at about five minutes to eight. When Mike Wallace closed, almost twenty minutes later, Justin turned the television off and sat for two minutes catching his breath. Abruptly he rose, descended the sixteen floors, and left the hotel, turning right toward Park Avenue. He continued walking west toward Broadway and thought foolishly to himself that he would surely be stopped on the street. *"That's the young man who is the son of Senator Castle!"* Absurd, such self-consciousness, he reproached himself.

Ridiculous. He wandered up Broadway to Lindy's on 51st Street, sat at the bar, and ordered a beer. It helped him take his mind off his own affairs to wonder if he might be sitting on the very same stool the columnist Victor Riesel had occupied the night the vengeance-bent union thug sprayed acid in Riesel's face. Justin closed his eyes to visualize the scene he had read about in journalism class. That happened—he forced himself to do the subtraction—thirty-five years ago. He asked the menacing bartender if he knew where Riesel was sitting. No luck. The bartender's mind wasn't on Victor Riesel.

Justin's heart was still beating fast, and soon he put down the beer to look at his watch. He would appease his self-concern by making sure to be back in his hotel room to hear the eleven o'clock news. On CBS there would surely be something on the subject of Senator Castle and the exposure of his . . . bastard son. He might as well get used to people denominating him in that way, though in fact his father and mother *were* married when he was born, so he was not a bastard. But he would need to explain his surname, Durban.

There was indeed mention on the eleven o'clock news of the *60 Minutes* exposé. The life and expected presidential candidacy of Senator Reuben Castle were featured, and the revelation of his early secret marriage and the son who had been born unacknowledged. The segment closed by quoting the statement being given to anyone who had dialed the senator's Washington office in the last couple of hours. *"Senator Castle has no comment on the false allegations made on the CBS program* 60 Minutes." There was no mention of the press conference scheduled for the next day, at which the announcement of the candidacy had been expected.

Justin pulled the blank ticket from his pocket.

Good time to visit Hawaii!

He wished he had a girlfriend to talk to. Could he order up a girlfriend? he found himself wondering. He thumbed through the bills in Mr. Wilson's envelope. Twenty twenty-dollar bills. Not much of a girlfriend there, the cosmopolitan twenty-one-year-old reflected wryly.

He could of course write down Boulder, Colorado, as the destination on his ticket. But there must at this point be much turmoil at home. Or he could write South Bend. Or...

He picked up the phone and dialed his own number at Notre Dame.

Allard answered. He told Justin excitedly that two reporters had come by wanting to know how to reach him. "I told them I didn't know where you were. They asked if I had seen *60 Minutes*. I pretended I hadn't. I wasn't about to tell them you had left a message for me to tune in. One of them—young guy, bien jeune—left his card. He wrote on it. Hang on. —Here. His name is Andrew Bjorn. B-j-o-r-n. He's from AP, gives an address in

Chicago. He wrote, 'Give me a ring. Important. Tonight.' It's an 800 number."

"What about the other guy?"

"The other guy was a she. A great big she, from the *South Bend Tribune*. I thought she was going to park down and sleep here till you got home. I got rid of her only ten minutes ago, told her you were probably headed to Boulder. Eh bien, Justin. Que faire?"

Justin waited a few moments. He was all but speechless with gratitude that Allard hadn't dived into questions about *60 Minutes*.

But then, everything about Allard was very special. Yes, he had been caught plagiarizing, and atoned for it by taking a month's probation and—his private spiritual expiation—denying himself golf for one month.

Justin now spoke to his friend in French. What would he say to a week in the woods in North Dakota, hunting and fishing?

"Chouette! Encore une semaine de vacances!" Of course Allard would take the week away. And yes, he would arrange for Duplessis to take Justin's French class for a week. They discussed arrangements.

Justin wore the semi-tailored hunting coat his mother had given him on his eighteenth birthday. She had several times demanded that he put it on when friends came by, so they could admire the cut and the dark red corduroy and the leather trim. He missed his own twenty-gauge shotgun, with which he had hunted many times over the years in Colorado, Paul alongside with his own shotgun. Up until age eighteen, he actually kept count: twenty-two woodchucks, sixty-four squirrels, ninety-four quail, forty-four doves.

But he was excited as his first duck dropped and he was able to feel the extra charge and exult over the range given by the twelve-gauge, with its Number 6 shot load.

He and Allard felt such exhilaration the first day that they decided there and then to celebrate. They had brought down six birds and retrieved them with the help of Ansel Adams, the bird dog on loan from Eric's young law partner. They pulled off their heavy clothes and hung them up to dry alongside the kerosene stove. Avidly they welcomed the heat as the October post-dawn cold asserted itself.

Imitating the most florid French maître d'hôtel, Allard said, "And what would Monsieur le Chasseur desire as a first course?"

There had never been better food or choicer wines, they told each other as they ate their scrambled eggs and toast, and they didn't wake until mid-afternoon, in time for the three-mile walk to the river, and the frigid stillness of the two hours spent enticing trout, and then the walk back to the duck blind and a quick restocking of the kerosene in the heater.

They napped for one hour, then set about cleaning and cooking two ducks.

Allard said, "What have you heard from Commander Belcourt?"

"Nothing. Well, yes, something, via Mr. Monsanto, our host. I was with him for an hour before meeting you at the airport."

"You didn't say anything, and that was the day before yesterday. So I thought I'd wait, see if you could bring down a duck. We can talk about ducks, if you like."

Justin poured two glasses of Chianti.

"What he said—what Mr. Monsanto said—was that a buddy in Winnipeg tipped him off that they were putting pressure on the arsonist, putting pressure on him for information they could use to track down the moneyman, the guy who put him up to it. Belcourt is threatening to charge the arsonist with felony murder, but hinting he might ease up on that a bit if he names the instigator of the fire. As of that morning, it hadn't worked. There is a problem—that the arsonist has been in and out of provincial prisons most of the last twenty years. If the Mounted Police wanted to pack him away for good, it's as easy as charging him with parole violations. So they don't need the Saint Anne's fire for extra pressure. And they don't hang 'em any more—right, Allard?"

"Right, Justin. That's a terrible pity, isn't it? Wish we could blame it on the pope, but Manitoba beat John Paul to the abolition of capital punishment by a dozen years."

"Manitoba is *so* civilized, Allard. I guess I never told you."

"Okay, okay. So, what is Commander Belcourt waiting for?"

"The arsonist to break down, tell him who hired him."

"This guy says he didn't do it?"

"Right. And Belcourt's case is pretty circumstantial, though he's certain he's got the right guy. Meanwhile, Senator Castle issued his press release—"

"I didn't know about that."

"It was while you were flying here. He did a press release on one or two of the *60 Minutes* allegations. He said he had never even stepped foot in Saint Anne's Church in Letellier."

"Well," Allard said, "maybe that's right? There's no extant documentation on that marriage."

Justin crawled up from where he was seated with his wine

and the skinned duck and groped his way to his backpack. He came back with an eight-by-ten print stapled to a negative, and handed it over. Allard studied it for a moment.

"Holy smoke! So this is what they burned and killed trying to suppress! Who's seen this?"

"Nobody. I was prepared to show it to the *60 Minutes* people, but only if I had to. So—nobody."

"Not your mother?"

"No."

"Not Eric Monsanto?"

"Allard, you probably never heard of General Nathan Bedford Forrest, but I spent time on him in the Civil War course last year. He was a very colorful guy. When an aide asked him the same question again and still again, General Forrest said— I'll write it out for you in English. It doesn't work in French." Justin tore off the top of the shell box and wrote the graphic words: " 'I tole you twicet, goddamit, no.' "

Justin continued: "Nobody but you has seen it. And you know, what I'm thinking is...what good is it?

"Commander Belcourt is trying to find out who commissioned the fire. Who had a motive to commission that fire, Allard?"

"Your father?"

"That's right. Nobody else I can think of. So if I burn this, they can't use it in making a murder case against...my father. I kept him maybe from being president. Maybe I can now keep him out of jail."

He put the print and the negative into the roaring kerosene flame. Allard raised his wine glass, and bowed his head. "Tu es bon, Justin. Très bon, mon ami."

ACKNOWLEDGMENTS

This novel was written in Nassau, our adopted winter home. My Swiss passport, after forty-five years, was stamped NE PLUS SKIER — the dreadful fate that hits all skiers when their time has palpably come to do something else. In Nassau one can swim and sail and play tennis and golf, none of which attracts me any more: so this novel came quickly to fruition, from an idea I had long ago played with, the life of an American rake.

I am enormously indebted to Michael Seringhaus, who took a brief leave from his graduate studies in molecular biophysics and biochemistry at Yale. We had become friends aboard my boat, on which he had undertaken a summer's chores a couple of years earlier. His schedule permitted him to spend a month with us in Nassau furnishing ideas, corrections, and inspiration.

As is almost always so, the next step was to deposit my manuscript with Samuel S. Vaughan, who has invested literacy and spark and subtlety in more than thirty of my books. His patience and ingenuity keep me alive and, as will be acknowledged by readers of *The Rake*, my writings perdurable. I am ever so grateful to him.

Lois Wallace, my agent, gave the manuscript her usual sharp-eyed reading. Linda Bridges of *National Review* was helpful and wonderfully informed. Frances Bronson kept us all in order, and I thank her for her talent and patience and affection.

This is my first outing under the patronage of Cal Morgan, the talented executive editor of HarperCollins, who has provided many helpful suggestions.

—WFB
Stamford, Connecticut
January 2007